AFTERSHOCK

....

TOM BENTLEY

The Write Word
Watsonville, CA

The Write Word Publishing
Watsonville, CA 95076
www.tombentley.com

Publisher's Note: This is a work of fiction. Names, characters, places, and incidents are a product of the author's imagination. Locales and public names are sometimes used for atmospheric purposes. Any resemblance to actual people, living or dead, or to businesses, companies, events, institutions, or locales is completely coincidental. Except when I mess around a little.

Aftershock / Tom Bentley — 1st ed.
ISBN 978-1-77342-039-4

To my sweetheart Alice, who has undergone many temblors and rumbles throughout our long alliance, and who has stood her ground with humor and grace.

The happiness of most people is not ruined by great catastrophes or fatal errors, but by the repetition of slowly destructive little things.

— Ernest Dimnet

ONE

....

I was thinking about my Studebaker when the quake hit. Though it's not exactly a showstopper, it's a '63 Lark, and pretty sweet. The Studey was on my mind because a moment before the building went bonkers I'd been looking at Diana's legs. She was wearing one of those napkin-sized skirts she sometimes wears and her legs are all the way up to there anyway. I always try not to stare—I've perfected this method of looking off in a fake distracted way and then flicking my eyes back. I can get away with zeroing in on her without getting caught, I think. It was almost quitting time, and I wasn't paying much actual attention to anything.

So there I was standing in my cubicle holding some papers and Diana was standing at the copy machine in that skirt and I was thinking that maybe if those Nazi mechanics of mine would fix that problem on the Studey, this time I could finally ask Diana out without worrying that my car would stall at a light and maybe leave us in the Tenderloin without wheels and me looking like Doofus Number One. And then the quake hit.

I felt it in my stomach first, a kind of squeezy uncomfortable feeling, like riding on one of those old centrifugal-force carnival rides where you lean against a wall on a spinning, circular platform, and then the floor drops away while you spin faster, pinning you to the wall in an awful, verge-of-nausea way. I never liked those rides, really, but I would always ride 'em when I could. You can't be smart all the time.

So my stomach did a couple of pirouettes before I really even knew what was going on and then the floor started moving in a real greasy way, a kind of sliding, humping, fucked-up kind of way, and I was finally clued in that it was an earthquake—and that it was a big one. There seemed to be a second wave that had more kick than the first and then the building really stepped onto the dance floor. It swayed big-time, and I mean swayed like you've downed ten tequila shooters and slapped yourself in the temple with an unabridged dictionary. My heart was now hammering like a trapped animal was inside.

Now it's not like I'm a quake virgin or anything. I'm a California boy all the way, and have been through more than a couple shakers in my thirty-plus, including one in the 70s when I was staying in Santa Barbara where I watched a nearby hillside seem to turn to liquid—but that was just my eyes jiggling. And since I'd moved to San Francisco, I'd felt the earth skip a beat more than a couple of times. I've always sort of liked it—the land stretching its legs a bit and all. And now it was almost the 90s, and there hadn't been a real big bumper for a while. But this was different.

Different because Consolidated Leasing—yeah, that's where I work; could a business name be any more lame?—is on the eighth floor of a new building on the edge of downtown, and it's built to flex in a quake—and *man* was it flexing. But different yet, because even with the flex, even with me having rocked and rolled through my share of quakes, this shaker seemed special right from the get-go.

A jolt punched me into the edge of my cubicle, and I hit the corner about armpit height, hard, and then I stumbled to one knee. Though I pretty much forgot about scoping Diana, she was still right in front of me and I saw that she was clutching the sides of the copying machine with both arms, a love-death grip. From my angle it looked like the machine was actually lifting into the air a little, but maybe that's because I wasn't exactly the Rock of Gibraltar myself. Also from my angle I saw that her little skirt had hiked up even further so that I could see where the thighs of those fine legs moved right up into that round rump, which was covered by red panties. I filed that away in one of those micro-seconds because it's really no time for my standard lech act, considering that the office was in a state of total pandemonium, and I'm not completely convinced that the entire building wasn't going to go kablooey right down onto Market Street. I tried to shout something out to Diana, but it came out like a strangled little bark.

Cubicles playing bumper cars with each other doesn't give me a lot of confidence. Since our building was getting so loosey-goosey, and we were on the top floor, office goods were really starting to scoot around with each pendulum swing of the building. Two of the tallest filing cabinets toppled with a huge crash, but I could barely hear that because of the shouts and screams that were rico-cheting around the office. After I'd righted myself a little using my cubicle wall, the next round of building flexing took my monitor tumbling off my desk, and it exploded on impact. *The novel!* My novel, the only damn thing that's seemed real to me in the last year, was on that computer. What if it was trashed too?

When I whirled around to check out the computer itself, another tremor hit that seemed to run sideways from the direction of the first. I was plunked right down in the aisle between the cubicle rows so that I sort of fell on my back and my butt, with my legs a little in the air. That gave me a splendid view of some of the plasterboard roof panels of the acoustic ceiling above, which were now deserting the roof in droves and diving to the floor. I had to get out—fast—but I felt like I was moving in slow motion. The novel, damn. The building—double-damn!

I sprang up, but was staggered by a rolling motion of the building. I was kind of half-crouching, half crab-walking my way across the office because there were so many toppled things on the floor, and so much noise and dust. I couldn't see or hear anyone who seemed actually injured, but I wasn't sure. I was scared, very scared, and I could barely focus. I had to jump over the most egregious example of wretched corporate art that the office possessed (on a lease, of all things), which had fallen to its deserved death off the wall. It had been pierced by the weird sharp-edged desk lamp that one of the graphic artists had brought in to try and prove that she wasn't a corporate drone. I had a fleeting thought that I hadn't appreciated her creativity before. But no time for thoughts.

At least six people were crowded into the office's open double-doorway, seeking wall-joint strength like good Californians should. Unfortunately for them, that was also the primary office exit, leading to the elevators and staircases and what seemed now to be an impossibly long flight away from a building that was still rumbling like it was moving to a good belly laugh.

The bulk of the office populace was now pouring toward those open double doors, where that half-dozen of the first mad scramblers had fled. I was moving with the pour, in fact, kind of pulling on the shoulder of a guy in front of me for momentum, as the floors and walls did another little tango. The doorway people were half-crouching, some with arms entangled, all leaning on the person next to them, all wide-eyed and open-mouthed. They looked so scared that I had a new gut-clench of fear.

The doorway crew didn't intend to abandon their protected place in the doorway, but those intentions had to negotiate with those of the half-crazed stream of souls coming toward them who had no intention of remaining in the building. I glanced back at the cubicles, seeing two people from payroll standing wall-eyed in the aisle, while a rivulet of a toppled Sparkletts bottle trickled between them toward me. When I turned back to continue for the door, my boss Megan was standing in front of me.

In front of me doesn't quite explain it though. When I turned back toward Megan, I was wearing her like an apron, since I had turned holding both my arms out from my waist and she had moved with her arms up and forward toward me. Since she's about a foot shorter than me, just in turning around I ended up involuntarily clasping her to my chest, which surprised us both.

I grabbed her by the shoulders and screamed "Megan!" which was all I could manage. My ante was too high for her, however—she couldn't even speak. We've all heard that phrase "white as a ghost." Just another phrase that's lost its elastic—but Megan brought a rich new meaning to a poor phrase.

I didn't have time to think this, but just absorbed it: She was drained of color, paste-white, a fully credible white that would never pretend to be the pallor of a living being. But I did detect a little pinkness in the center of her face: her tongue, usually as discreet as all of Megan's doings, now blatant because she was unable to engage it to make conversation. It rested limp on the bottom of her widely open mouth. Behind the heavy black horn-rims of her Elvis Costello glasses, Megan's bright blue eyes shrieked the words her tongue couldn't manage.

I did a little *pas de deux* with her in the aisle, spinning her by the shoulders toward the exit. In thinking of it afterward, I longed for a video: my formidable boss, always cordial but always reserved, impenetrable and boss-like, spun like an addled child and pointed toward the door. "I think we should get out," I said in as manly of a voice I could muster. But I was feeling some panic; my heart hadn't let up, and for a second the pounding made me think I was having a heart attack.

We were near the tail end of the crowd moving through the doorways. The first human wall of resistance clinging to the entryway had been breached—and like bowling pins, most had scattered, choosing the staircase path preferred by the bulk of those in flight. Probably two minutes, three at most had passed since the initial shock hit, and the building still seemed to be reverberating, though I couldn't judge time or the trembling with any accuracy.

I shepherded Megan past the lone doorway holdout, Squink from Accounting. He was gripping the doorsill with both hands, his eyes wet and dreamy as we went by. It was lucky I had Megan to tend, because that responsibility calmed my brimming panic.

"Squink, better head down. Maybe the worst of it's over," I said as we passed him. I thought I was getting the hang of this whole leadership-in-a-crisis thing, what with Megan acceding to every tiny pressure of my arm, and me feeling like most everything's in control. It was only when my knees buckled at the first staircase step that I realized that my whole body was slightly quivering, and that I had lost that fine motor control needed for precise movement.

I grabbed the handrail to steady myself, though Megan, in full zombie mode, didn't notice my stumble. At that moment, she might not have noticed if I had a long scaly tail and flippers. We merged into a mass of semi-orderly building deserters, moving haltingly down the staircases mostly three abreast. I saw Diana ahead of us, looking back with an alarmed look and then lurching forward. My crew, Silvie and Crenshaw, was ahead of her—I could see Silvie throw her arms up while she talked to Crenshaw as they descended. She had a characteristic way of flinging her arms about; she always wore about twenty bangles and wrist bracelets on each arm that clicked and clattered when she jostled them. I was glad to see they were both all right.

The only person I could see that had an injury was Mr. McManus, the portly Vice President, who had a pretty good gash on his forehead, against which he held a bloody handkerchief. There was a lot of tangible tension going down the stairs, which was a process less than brisk. "What if there's another quake? We're going to get squashed here!" someone said. "God, I wonder what my house looks like? I just put all this decorative glass on shelves in my living room," somebody else answered. "Goddamn. I thought the whole goddamn building was going down! The whole damn thing!" said one of the lawyers, who'd just come into the office before it hit. I had a strong urge to push everyone out of my way and rush down the stairs. *Calm down,* I said to myself. But I was anything but calm.

We came to the seventh-floor landing, where we met a surge of employees from the big insurance firm that worked there. I could see a couple of women who were crying, and several people who looked disheveled and shaken up, but no major injuries. An older man in a suit was standing on the side of the stairwell saying over and over, "Just move slowly and watch out for your neighbor. It's OK, move slowly down and watch out for your neighbor."

Just a few steps ahead someone I didn't know had a portable radio pinned to his ear. "Seven-point five! They're saying seven-point five, and major damage in the City. Big fires in the Marina. Not certain where it actually hit yet." We were slowing way down on the stairs as we came in contact with people emptying out of the sixth-floor offices. People were getting more anxious, pushing a little, and I could see a big guy ahead of us trying to force his way through. I felt a strong pressure in my gut, and tried to push back against it. But when I looked down at Megan, she looked weirdly calm. Some color had started to come back into her face.

"Megan, are you feeling better? You OK?"

She turned to me and nodded and softly said, "Yes." Her eyes still looked as if their owner was off vacationing, but at least she resembled the upright—if not uptight—boss that I reported to that morning. I turned into a bit of a robot myself after that, just moving kind of numbly with the crowd, listening to people speculate on what had happened, the fear squeezing their voices. But I kept jerking a bit as I went down the stairs—as we walked, it felt like there were more aftershocks, but I think my body might have been having little fear spasms. I couldn't tell.

A picture of my house on fire zipped through my mind. Sure, it was a rental, so it's not my house, but it had been hard enough finding the place after I left Santa Cruz in such a hurry a year before. It's a big Victorian, with a huge bay window in the Lower Haight. I hoped Drew, my housemate, hadn't been standing in front of that window debating his next decorating move. We hadn't lost any windows in our office, but I was plenty worried that big old house wouldn't have flexed quite like our spiffy new building.

It might have been thirty, forty minutes to get down to the lobby—it seemed like hours. Then, suddenly, we burst out onto Market Street. The noise was the first shock. The combined sounds—shouts, crashes, horns, machine noises, police sirens—hit with a physical impact, so that I ducked a little when I stepped out onto the street. It was pandemonium. I felt terrified all over again. The street and sidewalks were teeming with people, some milling about, some standing alone, many walking in waves up and down Market.

Traffic was completely stopped, with some cars left at odd angles in the middle of the street. I saw an empty Muni bus almost sideways, straddling both lanes with its door open. There was smashed glass all over the place, much of it from sidewalk-level storefront windows. Police cars were parked or in movement in all directions. I saw water gushing over a low rooftop wall and down the front of a nearby five- or six-story building onto the sidewalk below. Then I watched an ambulance pull up on the sidewalk of the building right next to ours and spill out its attendants, who rushed inside. I could hear sirens near and far. I noticed the big office building right across the street—it had thick white smoke pushing out of broken windows on the third floor. It was madness. I was breathing very fast, in short gulps and gasps.

People from our office had gathered in a loose circle on the sidewalk edge and in the street, trying to decide what to do. One of the sales guys was trying to get people to go to the Gnome's Hat, a dive bar around the corner, but nobody was listening. I thought I should try to call Drew at the house, but the only phone in sight had six or seven people crowded around it. I spun around in a small circle, looking up and down the street, and at my fellow workers, who didn't seem to be able to put a plan of action together. Silvie and Crenshaw stood off to the side, Silvie waving her arms and Crenshaw sucking on a cigarette with fierce concentration.

Then I noticed Megan staring at me. Though her complexion was returning to normal, she still looked stricken. She looked at me steadily for a moment and then said, slowly, in a tight-throated way that made her words croak a bit, "Hayden, I would greatly appreciate if you would walk me to my apartment. I'm feeling quite ill." She fluttered her arm toward my shoulder, and briefly rested it there and then she looked away. I thought I could see her trembling a little.

"Well, that'd probably be OK, Megan. I'll just try and call my place from your house—I'm a little worried because it's an old building." I tried not to smile too broadly when I said, "I'm glad to see you're getting some blood back—your face was the color of printer paper up there."

She touched one of her earlobes, covering one of her tiny pearl earrings. "Well, that's probably true. This is my first earthquake, and I'd like the number to stop there." She looked out at the crazed street scene and shuddered a little. "At the moment, I think I'd take the peril of Boston drivers over San Francisco earthquakes hands down."

Megan had come to Consolidated from Boston only two years before. She'd been an editor there, but also (because it was a small company) the Traffic Manager or some such ungodly title at a small boutique publisher in Boston, routing manuscripts, messages, contracts and communications through that office and across that quadrant of the East Coast's literary world. She did have all kinds of exchanges with agents and name authors, but that didn't count much at Consolidated. But damn, that contract work did: Now she ensured that leases had signatures, executives had quarterly reports and that meetings had 100% attendance. Consolidated leaned on her small frame with a vengeance, but she never seemed to be caught with a contract—or a sandy-blond hair—out of place.

First things first—get off of Market Street. I knew Megan lived somewhere on Taylor in Russian Hill, so I figured we'd walk up to California and maybe move north on Stockton, skirting Chinatown. I knew that would first take us through some of the big-boy buildings in the financial district, but I didn't want to flank the Embarcadero—I'd remembered that big waves can follow an earthquake, and though that seemed pretty unlikely in the Bay, I'd always had a strong fear of drowning. Megan still seemed only semi-coherent, so I just gestured the way with a pointing index finger up the street, and we moved through the chaos. I kept looking up at the tops of the buildings, expecting something to fall on us.

We started walking up to where California hits Market and I saw Leg Man, in his usual spot, not far from Consolidated. I saw him almost every morning, since he set up shop near the coffee stand where I regularly fueled up. Leg Man was a homeless guy, or at least he looked like a homeless guy, and like many of the homeless on Market, he had a regular spot where he plied his trade. The ways the homeless folks hit you up for dough on Market Street varied: some would try a story on every passerby, walking with you a bit to fast-talk a dollar. Some had crude or artistic signs with jokes on them—"Homeless man needs money for college and beer," or sad descriptions of their plight. Others would just sit slumped on the sidewalk, not looking at the masses moving by, maybe with a plastic cup to take any donations.

Leg Man was different. Leg Man had an artificial leg that he set up on the sidewalk, and at the top of the leg, a little above the knee, there was a little platform and connecting bracket. He'd position a small metal can there for people to drop money in. He usually stood stock-still back off the sidewalk from his leg—he didn't seem to need the leg to stand—looking at everyone passing by, a small scowl on his face. He was late forties, maybe fifty, black, a big, stocky guy with a small afro of wild, graying hair. Today, amidst the madness, his leg was next to him against the storefront wall he normally leaned against. He undoubtedly knew that pickings would be slim on a day when the entire City was upside-down.

I gave him a nod, and his eyes tightened a bit, but otherwise, he gave me no acknowledgment. But he gave Megan a long, sharp look and then gazed down the crowded street. He'd seen me many times, but I never knew if he recognized me or not, though I'd pushed a buck his way a few times. I wondered for a second if he knew Megan, but then we turned up toward California.

TWO

....

On the morning of the quake, in a dingy sleeping bag underneath a cardboard tent stretched between two alley dumpsters, Jacob Reed wrestled with a dream. He was walking down Market Street on a hot, humid day. But it was Market Street unlike he'd ever seen it. All the big buildings were there, but they were completely overgrown with fantastically tall palms and heavy ferns. The sidewalk was swampy mud, with reedy grasses tugging at his boots. He still had his leg and he felt strong. But something was horribly wrong.

The VC. They had his children. They had his children and wouldn't give them back, unless he made a great sacrifice. He was marching up to the head of Market to offer them all he had, but as he moved forward, he began shrinking—he was getting smaller and smaller. And then the pain in his leg, searing ...

He shuddered to consciousness, breathing fast. The old sleeping bag covering his face felt like it was suffocating him, so he clawed it off and pushed up from the pile of papers and cardboard. He rubbed his hand over his unshaven chin, and then pulled off the cardboard roof that he'd fashioned atop the dumpsters. *Ugly dream. The kids, it's been so long. But maybe they'd let down their guard and see me now—I've been steady for a while.* He stood and took a deep breath, thinking again of the children he hadn't seen in years.

But another sunny day, good. People give more on a sunny day. Maybe they're more relaxed, because they're warm. A body thing, more than a mental thing. He made a note to himself to check a sunny day's receipts against a cloudy one's. For this moment, the contents of the dream were whisked away.

Sunny but cool, at six-thirty in the morning. He rubbed his hands together to warm them and then rummaged around in his knapsack for the bag of trail mix he'd found yesterday in the trashcan right in front of the insurance building. *More than half-full. People throw away anything. Fools. Works out for me though. I'm just an old bird, eating seeds.*

He pulled the worn duffel bag he used for a pillow onto his lap, pressing low and firmly on the worn canvas, checking to make sure the leather money bag was still there. He felt its hard, squarish outline through the clothes surrounding it, and he grabbed it and transferred it to the backpack, as he did every morning before he went out to the street. He then settled back against the alley wall. *Probably have to go to the bank later in the week,* he thought. He grabbed the reading glasses from his knapsack and then the paperback.

The glasses, big black horn rims, looked small on Jacob's large, bony head. He had stolen them from a little drug store off of Seventh Street a year or so ago and had not long after vowed never to steal again. But he'd laughed about the little flutter of pride he felt in his declaration—more than most, he knew that control is had one day, lost another. His vow had stood one test: he'd been sorely tempted when a man had openly scowled at him when Jacob had asked for change. The man had then had accidentally dropped his wallet when he descended down the BART steps. Jacob stared at the wallet, fighting himself for almost five minutes before a knit-capped kid had scooped it up.

The paperback was a worn copy of *Wuthering Heights*. Jacob always read for a half-hour or so in the morning before he began his work, and this novel was as good as any. Along with the cover, the first 33 pages had been torn off, and the binding was loose. Jacob was up to Chapter 9, where Heathcliff disappears after Catherine accepts Edgar's proposal of marriage, but then she becomes ill, and marries years later. The language was a little high-flown for Jacob's taste, but the travails of the intertwined families fixed his attention. He suspected it would all come to a bad end.

He'd gotten the book from Sully, one of the younger bums who used the Woolworths on Market as the locale for his trade. "I got it from the dumpster behind the shop, but I never shoulda even bothered. Bunch a crap. All kinds of fancy-ass people with their bonny lass this and that. Words bigger than a stretch limo. Hell, it's supposed to be in English, but that spew's not English. *You* read it!"

Jacob had been a reader all his life, from flopping on the library floor for hours as a pre-adolescent, surrounded by sports biographies and dinosaur books, to more serious works—*Native Son, Invisible Man*—in high school in the late 50s. Now, reading in a cold alleyway posed no burden; he'd even carried a book or two on every march or action his squad took in Vietnam, catching pages at humid dawn or humid dusk when he could. Some books he read five, six times—war could be numbing in the bleak stretches of routine. And then hell would come, instant, ruthless.

He settled against the wall to read, sipping from the big water bottle he filled every night from the restaurant tap in the alley a couple of blocks down. The city was waking up: the Munis began to run more regularly after 6:30, with the ambitious office early birds often arriving before 7. He thought he might have heard Dexter blowing some low, rumbling tones on his sax a few blocks down, where a high hollow in the marble facade of the utility building gave his notes a fullness. He used to work near Dexter, until he noticed that his daily take was dimming while Dexter's was brimming. Besides, Dexter had started to blow some of that 70s and 80s fusion garbage. Leave Bird for Chick Corea? That's nowhere. Miles was messed up.

Jacob read for a while, thinking that Heathcliff's violent nature probably wouldn't get him the love he craved, no matter how he forced the issue. He put the book back into his knapsack and then strapped on the fake leg. His joint only ached a little—it might be a good day. He stretched, feeling the tightness in his shoulder where he'd taken a tracer those years ago. It had just gone in and out, but had torn up some tissue and left a little ball of scarring deep inside. At the time, he thought that the bullet was the worst thing that would happen to him that day, or any day, but that thought would turn out to be wrong. He stowed the duffel in the alley electric-circuit box he'd discovered had a bad lock and closed its small door.

He walked out in front of the big insurance building, spotting the budding stream of businesspeople, many of them whom looked like kids playing dress-up. Young men and women with confident walks and clean clothes, pushing forward. He settled by the edge of the building, out of the main traffic flow, where the cops usually wouldn't bother him unless they had a bug on. He unstrapped the artificial leg, set it up a few feet from the building's façade and put the cup on the connective joint at the leg's top. He moved back with his cane, and leaned against the wall.

Most people would look at the leg, squint or frown in non-recognition, and then catch its fact when they glanced up at Jacob against the wall. The biggest percentage would hurriedly look away, moving at a slightly accelerated clip. Some people would look at him gravely, sadly and move on. Some were visibly disgusted. Over time, Jacob had begun to study his clientele, noting reactions, gestures, words. *Marketing. That's what it's about. Making a brand. Work is a process. Always selling. Got to have a method, an approach.* He didn't use the leg for the first few years, and then he tried it, stopped, and began again, having calculated his returns. Now the leg was his signature.

He used to have a sign that said "Vietnam vet could use a little luck" or some variation, but that didn't seem to get him any more trade, and he started to tire of the long, wandering conversations he had with other passing vets who wanted to talk about their tour. He had talked about it as much as he could stand. He was through talking.

A short man with slicked-back hair walked by and tossed a coin into the cup, not looking at Jacob. *There's my shill, he thought. My rainmaker. Now let it flow.* Sometimes just one person putting a coin in could start a line of falling coins. People were robots sometimes, sheep, following the leader. Jacob occasionally put a few coins in the cup himself to warm it up, to kick-start the day. Sometimes he might make 30 bucks in a morning, sometimes 30 cents. You could never tell.

There was the blond, the one with the glasses like his. He'd seen her many times, particularly since he'd been steady here for months. She always carried that black, bulging briefcase, always looked in a hurry, always seemed distracted by something. But there was something else, something that he'd caught the last couple of times he'd seen her, but he couldn't quite place it. She reminded him of somebody, or something. Or there was something in the way she carried herself. But who, what? He hardly knew any young white women anymore, not since his college days after the war, and how many years ago was that? Hell, he hardly knew *any* women anymore. But he recognized something about her.

He watched her come into his line of vision, and she flipped a glance at him, their eyes meeting. *What is it? Can't quite place it. Something about her, though.* It's not like she'd remind him of his daughter—she's too old. White besides. His daughter Tabby would be almost 19, the same age he was when he went overseas. His son Joshua nearing 14. It had been eight years, many of them drunken ones, since he'd seen them, five since he talked to them. It seemed like a hundred. More limbs gone missing.

Someone put a bill in his cup while he was thinking of his kids, and Jacob hadn't seen who it was. Probably the tall guy with the nice suit and the cane; he'd glanced back at Jacob and given him a quick nod. Jacob liked to guess the occupation of his customers, or speculate on what they might say to themselves—"This week's good deed"—when they put a coin in his cup. *That one's a money man. Stocks, maybe. Probably trying to work some good ju-ju on his picks by giving the bum a bill. Whatever.*

It turned out to be a pretty good day. He'd collected seventeen dollars by 1pm, as well as a beautiful old silver cigarette case that he could probably pawn, handed to him without a look from a tall, silent woman. And a very good avocado and cheese sandwich given to him by one of his regulars, a rotund, fussy man with a little moustache who reminded Jacob of Oliver Hardy. He went back to the alley and checked on his sleeping bag, and then relaxed in the sun while he ate his sandwich. He fingered the silver case and tried to remember the last time he'd had a cigarette. It was before he'd stopped drinking—this time, actually stopped—and when he'd decided to start saving the money. Must be a good five years. *Funny how the cigarettes had been no sweat. But the booze. Not so funny.*

It was around five when he thought he'd pack it up, maybe walk up to the waterfront to look at the bridge and the rush-hour traffic. He'd strapped on his leg and slung his backpack over his shoulder when the strange rumbling began. *What the hell?* Then the quake kicked hard. Jacob went down on his bad leg, which was good, since the kneecap that hit the ground was plastic. At first he thought a shell had hit, and he had a brief flash of the smell of cordite. *Shells, crap, no cover!* A nearby woman fell against a sidewalk coffee cart and screamed—Jacob heard the screams of a patrol buddy whose intestines flopped completely out of his belly when a big slag of shrapnel had hit him. But what was falling wasn't shrapnel; it was glass from some office windows above. Jacob pushed up heavily to his feet and moved forward toward the edge of the sidewalk, but he had to quickly draw back, because a taxi hit the curb and ran up against a big newspaper stand right in front of him. Jacob pawed for the .45 strapped to his hip, but 20 years separated him from that gun. *Quake! That's it! Big one. No shells.*

Some people on the street tried to duck into the archway of the insurance building at the same time some tried to flee from the lobby, and they collided at the doors, cursing and shouting. When another shock hit, Jacob saw a bike messenger hit an old woman at pretty high speed, sending both of them hard to the ground. He started to run, but where? Somewhere above him, he heard a wrenching crack like tearing metal. *What's that? Snipers too? No, no, the quake.*

Market Street was in high panic—people running a few steps, stopping, and then looking for somewhere to go. Jacob's heart thudded heavily in his chest. He stepped forward, then backed up, and spun around. He felt like he was under attack, with no cover. His face was wild, eyes wide and mouth wide open.

Many people had left their cars, some after hitting the car ahead or being hit from behind. *Not good, not good, this isn't good. This is a bad one, not good.* A trolley line about twenty feet from Jacob had snapped, and it was sending sparks into the street. A dazed man was about to walk into it before Jacob shouted, "Look out! Live wire!" at him. The man looked wide-eyed at Jacob and wobbled away.

Jacob thought to check on his duffel, but reconsidered. The high windows that looked down on the alley might be raining glass. *I could die out here! But where is it safe?* He strode to the edge of the sidewalk. A few emergency vehicles appeared on the streets from different directions. Cops too, in numbers, but there was nowhere normal to park in the madness, so they left their cars wherever they could, at crazy angles. People moved out of the insurance building, raggedly, steadily, so Jacob moved to the side, rapidly looking all around him, left to right, up and down. All the buildings were bleeding their occupants, some of them crying, some shouting. The noise was engulfing, penetrating Jacob's skin.

The blended shouts, wailing sirens, gushing water, the crack of falling rubble, the crash of breaking glass and booming, unidentifiable industrial sounds waxed and waned for twenty, thirty, forty minutes, the broken buildings settling and sighing, with Jacob trying to stay out of the fray. *How can I help? Cops and medical folk everywhere, looking as confused as me. I'm probably just in the way. Damn, this city took a hit. Wonder how Sully is. Dexter. Damn, not good. And what about Tabby in Santa Cruz?* He involuntarily gulped a deep breath when he thought of his daughter. *But Santa Cruz is a long drive from this quake. I hope.*

He was backing quickly away from some running emergency personnel when he spotted the blond woman and a tall dark-haired man leaving the building together. She was very pale, and seemed lost. He thought that the man with her gave Jacob a little nod as he passed, but he wasn't sure. Jacob had seen him before; maybe he and the blond worked together?

Maybe that's the last of the shocks. Have to walk right down the center of the street to duck any falling crap. He started to walk to the waterfront anyway, to see how things looked out on the Bay Bridge. He thought of his daughter, and of his son. *Hope everybody's safe at home.*

As for his home, home could wait—even in an earthquake, an alley only moves a little.

THREE

....

E arly on the morning of the quake, Megan's work prepa-
rations had begun. Her rituals didn't vary: In the shower,
the cold water hit her skin with icy pinpricks. Though
giving herself a cold blast was how she started every shower of
every working morning, she still drew back in shock from the water's bitter embrace.

Despite the flushing in the shower, her mouth still felt stale and
dry. She exited the bath and toweled off, rubbing the thick, fluffy
towel under and around her breasts, lingering. The bathroom was
filled with steam. Megan leaned against the tile, sliding the soft
fabric up and down her belly and thighs. Then she straightened
and shook her head. No time to start with that, she thought; I've
barely got enough time to clean up.

She moved into the kitchen while putting on a red silk robe, and
felt the echo of a headache at her right temple. Megan winced at
the crushed cigarettes in the ashtray at the sink; she immediately
sealed them into a plastic bag and threw them in the trash. She
quickly washed the ashtray and put it in the dish drainer, which
was mostly filled with glasses and a couple of plates. The empty
bottle on the sink was whisked into the recycling box. She lifted

another to see its level in the light. She shook her head and put it in the side cabinet, where it clinked against some other bottles.

The Delderhurst contract probably has to go back through the lawyers today, she thought. *And I've got to call Chicago about those final negotiations for the cubicle sets. What's that vice-president's name? Klempsten, Kelmstein? Oh, I'll get it from my notes.*

She walked to the stately, scarred armoire in her bedroom and selected a gray, pinstriped pantsuit. Three meetings today—better look smart. She put her hand in one of the jacket pockets and retrieved a black plastic bottlecap. *Well, that's careless,* she thought, and tossed it into the wire basket in the bedroom. She moved into the living room, and squinted at the bright fall sunshine that flashed through the big double-windows looking out at the Bay. Alcatraz hunched in the distance, with the edge of the Bay Bridge to the east. A ferry moved slowly toward the East Bay, probably taking some commuters to their offices. *Another sunny day. My delphiniums—they might be dry. Dad would never let that happen.*

She walked to and through the terrace door and up the inner staircase that led to the building's roof. Though she shared the top floor with three other apartments, she'd never met any of her neighbors—or indeed any of the six-floor building's apartment residents—while up on the roof. Today would be different. When she exited the short, enclosed hall that led onto the roof, she saw a gangly man standing by the edge of the rooftop wall, staring off at the Bay. He whirled around when he heard the door shut.

"Well, OK! Howdy neighbor! No man is an island, eh? This your stomping ground up here? First time up for me. Name's Tuttle." He took a couple of quick, large strides up to Megan and thrust out a long, skinny palm, touching the bill of his worn cap with the other. Megan drew back a little but then put out her hand. "Excuse me, you startled me. Yes, I do. I mean, I do spend some time up here. I'm Megan Thornstock, 6C. I presume you live in the building?"

The man grinned widely and seemed to pat his stomach, though he didn't make contact with his body, and then he pointed down. "Sure, sure, eight months now. 3A. Three's a charm. Love the city, love the view. Been out here in California two years now, from Iowa, Des Moines. You sound like you aren't from these parts yourself."

Megan wished she hadn't chosen this moment to come up to the roof. She enjoyed the anonymity of the apartment house, and how to this point she'd only exchanged bland pleasantries with the neighbors she crossed entering or exiting the building. "Yes, that's true. I'm actually from London. London, England," she said, glancing quickly at the man's eager, open face. He was approaching forty, though there was a youthful, impulsive quality in his tone and movements. "But I've been here over twenty years," she added.

"Twenty years, shoot! Right here in this building? Good gosh Almighty, you're practically a native. Guess I can rely on you to point out the best bars and restaurants and the like, huh? You must know 'em all."

Megan tightened her lips. "No, I'm sorry, I don't frequent bars. Pardon me, Mr. Tuttle, I've enjoyed our conversation, but I really must tend to my garden, and then hurry to work, so if you'll excuse me ..." She turned away from him and toward the reason that had brought her to the roof.

"Shoot, you mean you did all this? Damn, that's great! Maybe I could even plant a little sweet corn up here to diversify your crop. Whew, you really did some work up here."

They were both facing Megan's garden, though they saw very different things. She had purchased a yard of grassy turf—though she referred to it as *sod*—and built up its earthen base with a foot of soil, and boxed it in a wooden frame. She'd positioned it against the enclosed staircase that led down from the roof, both for wind protection and its south-facing orientation. Her father had taught her well.

This green patch she bordered with various flowering plants, the delphiniums prominent among them. Nearby, she'd also built a small arbor about five feet tall, and had trained several varieties of roses, Jayne Austins and Jude the Obscures among them, to stretch up over and down its arch. (She'd forgiven the rose's developer the miscasting of Austen's name.) She had positioned a lounge chair and small table nearby to view the garden's glory at her leisure.

It being late fall, the border flowers were a little rough, but some of the roses still held bright color. She approached her plot, stuck a finger in the ground to test for dryness, and then grabbed the hose to spritz the soil. *Maybe he'll go away now. Could he have been serious about the corn?* But Tuttle was enjoying the view and the company. It was Tuttle who first spotted the book.

It was *Wuthering Heights,* flopped open at the spine, under the little table. A tipped-over plastic glass was nearby. The novel wasn't one of her precious first editions, but a nice leather-bound volume nonetheless. It was damp from that morning's dew. He picked it up and flipped through its pages, and rubbed some of them with scrutiny, a look of concentration on his face.

"Well, I'm guessing this is yours as well. You're probably the literary type as well as the gardening type, huh?" He glanced at the toppled glass and said, "A little snort makes every book better, sure." He looked the book over again and said, "No worse for wear, but it ain't gonna be easy on the pages after a few more nights out here."

Megan twisted from her watering and winced at Tuttle's handling of the volume. She turned off the hose and stepped quickly to him, reaching for the book. "Thank you very much, Mister Tuttle. Yes, the book's mine, yes, thank you."

"Right you are," he said, handing it over. "But it's not Mister Tuttle, it's just Tuttle. My last name is Turknot, Tuttle Turknot. Pleased to know you." He again thrust out his hand, and again Megan gave it a brief shake.

"Mr. Tuttle, I mean, Mr. Turknot, I don't mean to be rude, but I really must get ready for work. It was a pleasure meeting you. Goodbye."

"Pleasure it was, it was. I hope we can trade some gardening tips sometime. I know a lot about turnips too."

She turned and walked to the staircase entrance, looking down at the book. *How could I have left this up here? It must have been the other evening, when I'd left work early for the dentist appointment and was relaxing a bit afterward. Ah, Emily, forgive me.* She glanced back at the tipped glass, shook her head, but then moved purposefully back down into her apartment. *That man, dear Lord ... gardening tips.* She shuddered and let out a long breath. She slipped the book halfway into the great bookcase that dominated one wall of the small living room, but then withdrew it, and set it out on a coffee table to fully dry.

The sunlight filled the room, glancing off the white walls, and illuminating the fine crown molding at the juncture of wall and roof. The building's apartments had been well cared for—the one-foot high ornamental frieze integrated into the molding ran through all the rooms; it had been the dealmaker for Megan's rental of the apartment. She'd thought of it as a novel on the walls, delighting in the fine detailing of the Renaissance characters, shown in all aspects of daily life. She'd mentally composed elaborate tales about selected characters, assigning the souls of star-crossed lovers, scheming merchants and meddling parents to her favorites. She left the building worrying that Mr. Turknot might slip up to the roof with a wheelbarrow of seeds.

She was lucky enough to get a seat on the Muni, and was able to refresh herself from her day planner on the details of the Delderhurst deal, which had to be attended to immediately upon arriving at the office. She almost missed her stop at the top of Market because she was calculating some accelerated interest rates on a lease for a fleet of limousines she was researching for a corporation in Kansas City.

Right when she was pulling open the big glass door at Consolidated she noticed the grizzled black man hunched over against the wall of the building, coughing into an old bandanna. He looked up at her just as she looked at him. *Oh, there's that disabled man again. He's so very unpleasant with that false leg of his. And his begging. It's sad. Could he have kids, be someone's father?* She moved through Consolidated's double doors, wondering when San Francisco would once again reform its vagrancy laws, which seemed to go from liberal to restrictive with each whip of the wind.

She promptly forgot about the beggar when she entered the elevator, where Mr. McManus, Consolidated's Vice President, gestured for her to squeeze in beside him. He managed to make room where there was none due to the influence of his substantial bottom, with which he wielded glancing blows to the other elevator passengers to clear room for Megan. She inserted herself in the narrow gap between his huge hip and the lanky frame of a dreadlocked bike messenger, who was listening obliviously to music storming loudly out of the small headphones that barely contained it.

"Ah, bright and early Megan, bright and early. You're Consolidated's efficiency model, to be sure. Do you have a full plate today?" McManus leaned his head down toward Megan, releasing a cloud of garlic from that morning's breakfast.

Megan shrunk back as best she could, though she tried to avoid touching the bike messenger, who carried his own aroma, smelling to Megan of a ripe Stilton. "Yes, Mr. McManus, it will be another busy one. But I think we've got it under control."

"Capital, capital! A lease is no lease at all without control." McManus giggled a bit, jostling his bulk against Megan's mid-section. She grimaced, thinking of how many times McManus, who was from Toledo, affected a British accent or used what he considered to be Britishisms around her. But he wasn't alone among the broad American welcoming committee, who more than twenty years after her arrival in the country persisted in trying out their UK accents on her or making a remark about British food or repressed British manners. Megan usually left them to their idiocies, having discovered that no reaction prompted most boors to shift to their repertoire's next winning subject.

Her day moved through its usual motions: meeting, phone calls, spreadsheets, meeting, circulation of contracts, phone calls, meeting. In the mid-afternoon, she closed out the folder on one of the biggest leases the company had ever been involved in, a complicated office equipment deal with several subcontractors and sub-lessees. She put away the files with a small smile and even a little feeling of sentiment for a project's passing. But moments later, her mother called. Megan got up and shut her office door.

They exchanged the usual pleasantries, and then it began: "Megan, have you considered the situation we discussed during our last call? I've spoken to Professor Blakely several times since. He's assured me that your admission to the BU program is almost a certainty. He said he would put in a strong word to the admissions committee. This is a rich opportunity, Megan."

Megan paused, and took a deep breath. "Mother, I don't wish to sound ungrateful—I really don't. But I've made my decision. I spent years in academic programs already, and I won't spend more. I am now a Californian; this is where I work, and where I live." She paused again, listening, but her mother said nothing. Then Megan said, "It's where I'm going to stay." She hesitated and then said, "But what does father think?"

Her mother's pause was longer. Finally she said, "It's a squandering, Megan. California—it's just beaches and those Hollywood people. That's not a culture. Your father and I didn't raise you to be surrounded by ignoramuses." Her mother's tone turned a corner into harshness: "Are you turning your back on your family?"

"Mother, your feelings about California come from magazine articles. Not to mention your circle of friends who can't see past their antiques and their boxes at the opera. There is culture here— I'd show you if you and father would ever agree to visit." She sighed aloud. Since she'd left Boston, her mother had been after her to complete the Ph.D. program in Elizabethan Literature at Boston University that Megan had abandoned. It had initially crushed her mother that she had pursued an MA at Boston rather than at Harvard. That loss of prestige was further soiled when Megan slanted all her classes toward the Brontes and Austen, and even—horrors!—modern Western literature and poetry.

Megan's mother had abandoned her own profound academic interests when she'd married her father, dropping out of an advanced degree program at London's King's College, where she'd breathed in Spenser, Marlowe and Shakespeare. She'd never fully expelled that breath.

"Megan, you know your father is much too busy with his lecturing to come out West. And goodness knows that he's knee-deep in his clocks."

"His clocks? What do you mean?"

"I mean that your father has filled his workshop with old clocks that he's been fussing with for the past six months, old watches too. He's moved half his gardening tools outdoors. I've never seen the roses look so weary. It's all I can do to just keep the garden tidy, much less flourishing."

Megan sat bolt upright in her chair. Clocks? Her father and clocks? "Mother, do you mean that father's abandoned his gardening for clocks and watches? It's inconceivable! Are you exaggerating?"

Her mother's voice came back more softly. "Megan, you know your father and his tangents. He'll return to the garden. But it's clocks for now. However, chatting about your father's hobbies wasn't the purpose of my call."

Megan slumped back in the swiveling chair. "Mother, let's discuss this another time. It's a very busy day for me. Please say hello to father. And remind him that I haven't heard directly from him in months."

"I will say hello to him. And it certainly hasn't been months. But I won't, and you can't, simply let this chance slip away. Remember, Megan, we only want the best for you."

Megan hung up and put her chin in her hand. *Only the best.* She frowned. *My father hasn't wanted anything for me or from me in years— I doubt if he's given me as much thought as the roses he's worshipped for thirty years. And now clocks. Watches.* She felt slightly nauseated, her gut churning. She swallowed, feeling parched, but the glass of water on the desk had no appeal.

She got up and left the office to check on some troublesome contract language with one of the lawyers. There was Hayden, the proofing coordinator, leaning over Diana's cubicle again. *He does seem to perform his work well enough, but it looks as though he flirts with the office personnel as much as works with them.* She nodded to Hayden as she passed him, and he took his arms off the cubicle's top and straightened as she moved by him.

"Not one misspelled word in any contract today, Megan. Not a period out of place. In fact, I'd venture that every punctuation mark in this office is earning its keep today," Hayden said to her back as she walked away. She turned and smiled, and moved on to her office. *He does have an extravagant sense of humor, though. I don't know if that's an office benefit or not, but it's probably harmless.*

An hour later, the quake struck. Megan was in her office bending down in front of an open filing cabinet when the tray full of contract documents on top crashed onto the floor. Without comprehension, she tried to steady herself on the cabinet, which toppled sideways. The tallest of the metal shelving behind her desk collapsed from within, so that the shelves flopped on top of one another in succession.

Megan let out a strangled yelp and drew back into the center of the office. *God, God, God, what is this, God! Earthquake, San Francisco earthquake, god damn it!* She struggled to walk, the office floor seeming to leap forward, and her legs buckled. When she first tried to pull open the office door, it wouldn't budge, but she was able to wrench it open on the second try.

She tottered into the central office hallway and toward the cubicle rows. It was chaos, filing cabinets, computer monitors, papers everywhere. Shouting, people shouting. She stood dazed, leaning against a disconnected cubicle wall in the main cubicle aisle. Then she saw Hayden, his back to her, who seemed to be calmly surveying it all. Hayden, she thought. He'll help. She walked up to him, shaky, arms stretched out like a sleepwalker.

FOUR

....

We trudged up California, not talking. I started wondering how trashed our office was. It might help to know that our office is not going to win any design awards for innovation or architectural flair or for that matter, the quality of its business concerns. Sure, it's an OK building at the corner of Market and Main, just off the Embarcadero. We lease big equipment to big companies. Big deal. If your company needs a fleet of trucks to shoot widgets from Daly City to Jersey City, we're in the book. If your five thousand employees need five hundred copiers, and you don't want to pay up front, we'll meet you around the back. And if you're a big wheel and you want to flash it, we'll even arrange for you to lease a corporate jet on the cheap—if you call thirty thousand a month cheap. Of course, we don't own any of this crap we lease anyway—we're just middlemen, picking up as much change as spills out of the pockets of corporate America on its way from here to there.

The office is modern enough, which is to say that that oatmeal-puke fur that lines the cubicle walls isn't torn—at least it wasn't until now—and the Sparkletts water bottles get changed on a regular basis. There are about thirty people that work in the office (and about twenty lawyers that work outside), and it's mostly a young bunch, though the sales guys have some mileage on their faces and plenty of air in their spare tires. But I don't deal with those guys anyway. I really only deal with the people in the so-called Editorial department, issuing decrees from my exalted throne as Proofreading Coordinator.

We do documents at Consolidated. Oh boy, do we do documents. Paper-industry bigwigs must rely on leasing contracts for their year-end bonuses. If your company wants to lease office furniture for a three-story building, the leasing contract might be a story tall all by itself. But that's not to say it's an *interesting* story. Contracts are about 98 percent fat, and that's all the boilerplate mumbo-jumbo that goes into all the contracts, whether the items being leased are tanks or tortilla chips.

We've got that phalanx of lawyers twiddling the same documents in twenty different ways depending on the piddling new info in the contracts, and since lawyers couldn't be bothered to spend any extra time exercising their eyeballs on the precious billable words they've inserted into the contracts, we need a whole crew— well, two, plus me to bless their sweaty efforts—to make sure that every T is not only crossed, but in the correct typeface, line length and proper page placement.

That takes an editor's eyes—though we call 'em proofers so they don't ask for raises too often—and those eyes must be overseen by yours truly, the executive editor, a title I no doubt deserve, but this being Consolidated, they act as though they'd conferred the Order of the Knights of Malta on me with my paltry present title.

Maybe the novel could change all that, but that seems like miles off. The fact that I have a Bachelor's in Philosophy (and even a year in grad school) doesn't seem to carry any pay-scale weight either. I try to be philosophical about it.

But you need something other than a philosophy degree to navigate post-earthquake streets. California was only marginally better than Market. The same twisted street scene of stopped cars, blocked drivers, bewildered pedestrians and buildings with some bites taken out of them. We headed into the living traffic, surrounded by confusion and crazy conversation. A story moved from behind us and forward through us, as though it were an electric shock: "The Bay Bridge collapsed! Whole thing's down in the water. Rush hour—can you imagine it?" It was truly surreal—not merely the thought that that huge structure over the Bay had fallen, but how there was a tangible feeling that the story was like a swarm of bees or wasps that moved electrically through the crowd, stinging people with news as they passed.

I didn't really believe the thing about the bridge, and was going to tell Megan as much, but when I looked at her, she just glanced at me with a look of such sick grimness that I didn't say anything. We hurried on as best we could, Megan clacking in her heels through the crowd. She was wearing one of those pinstriped, pant-suit kind of things she often wore, when she wasn't wearing a dress. I wonder if she even owned a pair of jeans.

On the corner of California and Kearny was a scene I won't forget: a middle-aged man was just turning around in a small circle, weeping loudly, and just a few feet away, a heavily tattooed woman who looked like a bike messenger was gesturing to the sky and laughing maniacally. It was hard to tell which one was in worse shape. We moved on.

We headed up Stockton and started to climb the hill. On the edge of Chinatown I saw a strange sight: there were a bunch of those pressed, flattened ducks that they sell in plastic bags spilled all over the sidewalk, along with a bunch of root- and twig-like things, some kind of loose tea or herbs. All of the display racks of the ducks and some of the shelves had flipped over and spilled everything, and a guy that looked like he might have been the proprietor was just staring at the stuff on the ground.

Weird that I was walking through all this stuff with Megan, my high-minded boss, in whose office you'd never find an errant duck feather, much less anything spilled. Not that I'm really complaining. In my storied history of bosses, I've had ogres, oafs and other assorted hind ends. Megan was the picture of reason, calm and cordiality.

I'd spent a few idle moments in the past wondering how Consolidated could have lured Megan out of her Boston environs. She seemed so quintessentially Right Coast and proper, a person who could probably get away with wearing white gloves to work without it seeming wholly absurd, someone who might not visibly stiffen if you spoke to her with food in your mouth, but whose delicate glance away would prompt that mouth's closing. Even though she was just a year or two older than me, her manner seemed ten. But maybe I'm not telling it right: It's not like she was a stiff—she was just someone you couldn't see getting loose. She wasn't stuffy in some dried-up way; she was simply precise. Her opinions—and her English—were never sloppy.

Maybe the source of that tidy English was the fact that she *was* English: she grew up in suburban London, an only child of well-to-do parents who left when she was nine, after her father accepted a position at a Boston law firm, while teaching law part-time at Boston University. Her mom had been born in Boston, but had met her dad in London. Suffice it to say that Megan was the only one I knew who had had a nanny. At the moment, both of us—and maybe even the City itself—could have probably used a nanny, but we would have to soldier on without.

We got over to Taylor and started heading north and up and if you know Taylor, you know I mean *up*. Taylor was quieter than the streets we'd passed, though there was full evidence that something had given the street a big shake. It was pretty close to dark now, and darker yet, because there was no power. It was quite eerie to ascend the street and come to corners where you could see toward downtown and the Bay. San Francisco with no lights was something strange, the tall buildings dark and brooding, with sirens still going off in every direction.

I was surprised at how well Megan moved in those heels up that hill. It's not like she's out of shape or anything; in fact, as I walked close behind her I found myself admiring the pull of her hips as she tackled that hill, with the street's angle and her motion tugging her loose pants so that they outlined her small, tight frame. I shook my head a little bit—I can't think of Megan that way, no. My mind quickly moved on to those red panties of Diana's I'd caught a glimpse of that morning. I was so deep into a warm thought about Diana that when Megan turned back to me and spoke I almost jumped.

"This is it—I'm on the top floor."

I glanced up at a five- or six-story apartment complex, *The Belvedere,* with its street address written out in script letters with a flourish. Russian Hill might only be five or six miles from my place in the Haight, but it was a world away as well. There was no obvious damage to the stately old building, though it looked like someone had stacked a bunch of cardboard boxes out front filled with broken stuff.

"OK. I probably should get over to my place and see if it's still standing. Take care, Megan."

I turned back down the hill and started off. Megan's voice behind me was too sharp for the short distance between us.

"Hayden! Hayden, maybe you could come up for a moment and help me determine if everything's all right. I, I think that I wouldn't be able to right my bigger bookcases if they've fallen."

She looked at me quickly and looked away down the street, her hand scratching a bit at her face.

"Well, yeah, sure. I mean, maybe just for a minute. I really should get home." Man, at the beginning of this day, could I ever have predicted I'd be asked into the boss's apartment that night?

All it took was a huge earthquake.

FIVE

....

S he opened the lobby door of her building and we went in, and I got creeped out immediately. Like I said, the Belvedere is an old, fancy building, another sterling example of cornices and buttresses and whatevernesses blathered about in those "architecture is art" magazines I see lawyers carrying on Muni when they want to demonstrate that they're sensitive. We're in this little lobby, more like a foyer, really, and it's all plaster flourishes and a couple of heavy wooden chairs and even a bust of some big-lipped Roman or Greek that no one in my Bakersfield high-school class could have named.

But that wasn't what creeped me out. It was that someone had duct-taped an "X" across the old elevator doors and for some stupid reason that immediately made me think that someone had died on the elevator that day. It didn't help that there was barely any light coming through the entryway now that it was almost completely dark outside.

I was following behind Megan, who had started toward a row of little mailboxes on the wall, but then she stopped and abruptly turned back toward me—almost running into me—when she saw the elevator. "The elevator, the elevator, shit. Oh, I'm sorry," she said. "I don't mean to curse, but what a day. I guess it's the stairway for us yet again. Top floor, sorry."

"Hey, it's not like I haven't heard that word before, no problem," I said. Though I'd never heard it from Megan. She was the only person I've ever heard use the expression "Drat!" without joking. We started going up a narrow white staircase with ornate rails when it hit me that I was marching right up to the top floor of a building after a big earthquake that had sent me flying *away* from the top floor of a building. And I knew that aftershocks were no joke—I thought I'd even felt a little one as we walked on California Street.

"Hey Megan," I said to her back as she quickly moved up the staircase, "Listen, I really will just peek in and help you check out your place, but you know, we need to be careful about aftershocks and everything."

She turned quickly around, with her one-stair height advantage putting us almost face to face. "*Aftershocks?* Well, that's not all that likely, is it? I mean, as big as what we just had? That's not really likely, correct?"

"Hey, I'm no scientist, but they do happen; I'm pretty sure I felt one while we were walking. Even though your building looks like it's OK, maybe being on the top floor isn't all that safe."

Even up close, I could barely make out her expression in the dim light, but her face seemed to flit from frightened to determined and back again. She turned away and started up the stairs again, though more slowly. "It has got to be safe," she said. "This is the only place in the city I have to go. It's safe."

I was going to point out to her that she could probably go to a hotel—it was obvious from rents in this part of town that a couple of nights in a hotel wouldn't bring her bank account to its knees. Even with the power out, there must be something open. But I just clammed up and kept climbing. She was still the boss, even after hours.

No one said anything the rest of the way up, though my heart was moving into third gear by the time we hit the sixth floor. I thought that Megan might be capable of running a marathon in high heels by the way she rabbitted up the stairs. She opened her apartment door, but didn't enter, leaning in to peer around, with me peeking in over her head.

"Dammit! Oh dammit, dammit, dammit! I knew it!" She moved toward the room's center, and I followed. It was pretty dark, though a couple of large picture windows admitted dim light, but that only from the waning sun, since the city was eerily black. We were in what had to be her living room, a big, high-ceilinged space that probably looked much better earlier in the day, when the huge wooden bookcase that was flopped over a coffee table had been standing upright. Megan was on her knees on the floor, tugging on a big hardcover book that was lodged between the table and the bookcase.

"Megan, hey, you're never gonna get that out. Wait." I went over to one edge of the bookcase and tried to hoist it up. I figured I'd display some more of the manly, "earthquake-ready" Hayden that I thought I'd pulled off at Consolidated, but I almost pulled my back instead trying to get that case off the table.

"Man, this thing's a beast! What's it made of, wood-covered marble?"

"No. Mahogany. Nineteenth century. It's a Jenkins—they also made coffins. Let me light some candles and then I'll help you with it."

She moved to what I suspected was the kitchen and then back to a little table on the side of the room. She set down three enormous candles, two of them on high metal stands, the kind of tapers you might see in your local cathedral. She positioned them on the edges of the room. Once they were lit, I could dimly see the fancy ornamentation on the wall panels, and see that the room was almost like a private library, though most libraries don't have most of their books scattered on the floor.

"Let's lift it together," Megan said. She moved to the other side of the bookcase, and we partnered it up, despite the fact that it looked about twice Megan's height. Two Megans could be buried in this Jenkins. Another big cabinet, just as tall but narrower, was flopped down on the other side of the room, and we did the same power-lift with that. In lifting both cases, we spilled more books onto the floor, which now resembled Librarian Hell. We nudged both leviathans back into place against the walls, and I stood back to survey the damage.

"Can you please start returning the books to the shelves? I would like a drink, and you're quite welcome to join me."

She nodded at me, nodded at the books and walked to the kitchen. I suppressed an urge to tell her that the workday was done, and kneeled on the floor to pick up books instead. The floor was an amazing show—the Strewn Female Pantheon, or something like it. The Brontes—all of them—were tumbled about like a family re-union gone awry. Every Jane Austen I'd ever heard of, every one I hadn't, and every critical essay about her that no one had ever read. A lot of Sylvia Plath, and much, much more *about* Sylvia Plath. And so many of the books were just *tomes*—heavy, hard-bound volumes that seemed so old and weighty that I wondered if my hands, hands that had enjoyed more than their share of Batman comic books, should even be touching these books.

It's not like I hadn't read literature, even some so-called women's literature. I remembered *Sense and Sensibility,* sort of. I remembered it was funny. Kind of funny, at least. I knew what the premise of *A Room with a View* was. Before I turned to philosophy, I'd majored in creative writing. I'm almost certain I even got laid once because I knew that Sartre's girlfriend was Simone de Beauvoir, and when I dropped that nugget, as casual as could be, in a college bar filled with liquored-up literary types, I soon had a frisky co-ed at my side who seemed to find my bon mots ever so charming.

But all these books—it looked like Megan should be teaching Comparative Girly Literature at some private college back east, not lining up the sitting ducks in contracts. I started putting the biggest books on the bottom shelf of the biggest bookcase when I thought I should ask her if she wanted it done differently. Then I started to imagine my book on Megan's shelves, next to all those gals. Or maybe my *series* of books. It had flitted through my mind for months that Megan's back-East literary connections might one day be my connections too.

I walked around the edge of the hall right when Megan, at the sink with her back to me, seemed to be throwing her head back in some kind of exercise routine. She turned toward me when she heard me approach, and even in the dim candlelight, I could see the shot glass in her hand.

"Hayden. Hi. Just mixing up the drinks. Here's yours." She handed me a highball glass with a swizzle stick topped by a tiny glass miniature book. "Vodka tonic. Hope you like vodka. Let's go back in the living room." I glanced around at the kitchen, which seemed to be in pretty good shape, though there was a small cabinet overturned with some broken glassware in front on the floor.

There were a bunch of pots and pans hanging from hooks against a wall—and a big one on the floor—and I had an amusing thought of Megan holding a large dinner party with dead literary luminaries from centuries past.

We moved back from the big kitchen into the living room. My eyes had adjusted to the light, and I could see that though a lot of stuff had either fallen to the floor from tables or shelves, or tipped over, not much was really damaged. No other obvious broken glass. The tallest bookcase did have a big gash in it where it had side-swiped the table, and the table bore its twin scar.

Megan gestured with her drink toward the big leather couch, while she darted around the room, straightening up. I spotted the phone over on a high wooden stand near a dining table. "Hey Megan, can I use the phone? I should call my housemates." I kept thinking of Drew, and even Roland, in our old house, and all that might have happened.

Busy with a dumped-over magazine rack, she gestured toward the phone, not saying anything. I tried my house, but only got that rapid busy signal that tells you there's some kind of phone problem. I went back to putting books on the shelf.

"You know," I said, "If you've read all of these, you're probably qualified for tenure at San Francisco State. Or at least as a visiting lecturer. Did you ever want to be a teacher?"

She snorted from across the room. "Teacher? God! My mother has wanted me to teach literature since before I was born. Thirty-four, and my mother still feels that I need her career guidance."

"Huh. Sounds like a drag. What did your father want you to do?"

It was like I'd asked her if she liked to lick the armpits of high-school football players. She stopped stacking some books at the narrow case, turned toward me, and said nothing. After a moment, she said, "That's a good question. Do you want another drink?"

"Nah, I'm still half-full, thanks."

She walked past me and back into the kitchen, where I could hear the ice cubes clinking. Little testy about her dad. Or something. My eyes wandered around the room, looking at the heavy furnishings—old-style boardroom, by my judgment. I lit on a clock radio, odd in this room of antiques, whose digital readout told me it was almost eight. Wait, that radio's working! I went over and picked it up, seeing that it was powered by batteries. I turned it on, and dialed in to KGO and immediately heard, "... centered in the Santa Cruz Mountains, 7.1 magnitude, with considerable damage to downtown Santa Cruz and neighboring cities..."

Santa Cruz! What about Sun? Sun, my fantastic, frustrating girl-friend of four years there, my half-hippie, half-Republican, all-crazy sweetheart, whom I'd angrily left well over a year ago to start a San Francisco, sans-Sun life. What if she was hurt?

"Megan, I really need to use your phone again, long distance. The quake was centered in Santa Cruz, 7.1. My girl—uh, my best friends are there and I want to make sure everyone's all right."

Megan came out of the kitchen, her glass full and frosty. "That's fine, Hayden. I hope you get through." She sat down opposite me in a high-backed leather chair, sipping at her drink. I rapidly dialed Sun's house, the numbers moving through my fingers without hesitation, though it had been a year since we'd spoken. Again, the same quick, pulsing busy signal.

"Damn, still messed up. Damn."

Megan looked at me with a small smile, and gestured at my almost-empty glass. "Let me freshen your drink," she said.

"Freshen your drink." It was a bridge-club kind of thing to say, not a natural phrase from one of my peers. I suddenly felt uncomfortable. "Megan, it's past eight. I really should go check on my house."

She cocked her head to the side and raised her eyebrows, a look that made me think of a comical cat. Her mood seemed to be improving. "I really don't want to hold you, Hayden, but I'm just now beginning to calm down after the quake, and your company has helped."

She got up and took my now-empty glass, and walked into the kitchen, saying as she went, "One more for the road, as some boorish barman must have once said. Besides, the ice cubes are almost all melted—shame to waste them."

OK. I really wouldn't mind another drink, though I couldn't quite breathe easy in this candlelit room—it felt like we were about to have a séance. And I was getting hungry. I put more books on the shelves, and worked on that for a while, longer than was necessary just to have a drink made. The time and the kitchen noise I heard were explained when Megan emerged with a big wooden tray with hot Chinese food on plates and fresh drinks for both of us.

"Takeout from last night," she said. "I'm not much of a cook, but there's a great restaurant on every corner in this area. Lucky I have a gas stove."

She set it on the coffee table and pulled the high-backed chair over, looking at me expectantly. I started to make some perfunctory objection to her making me dinner, but what the hell, I was hungry and here it was—not like it was some home-cooked meal on our third date.

I dug in, and gestured with my fork at the wall above her. "This is a pretty crazy room. Like all those figures and scenes on the wall—it's like some kind of Grecian comic book or something."

Megan put down her fork and looked at me. "The frieze is one of the reasons I moved in. It's hardly a comic book. Each of the scenes is a narrative, plotted much like a work of fiction."

I took a long pull of my drink. *It's your boss,* I said to myself. *Remember now, this is your boss, and the one with the publishing connections.* "Well," I said, pointing my fork to the floor, which was still strewn with books, "Fiction on the ceiling, fiction on the floor. You've pretty much got it covered, at least where the Women Writers of Centuries Past is concerned."

I thought that was pretty clever, and I laughed a bit, trying to keep my mouth shut so that no Chinese landed on Jane Austen. I might have been a bit premature—or immature—in my humor assessment.

Megan put down her fork and picked up her drink, a neutral look on her face. Then she straightened and looked at me. "Hayden, before you are some of the greatest works of literature ever written. They are timeless. Do you even have a passing familiarity with literature? Or is your reading confined to poring over leases at Consolidated?"

Her tone had chilled considerably, but I could compete. I put my fork down, and took a sip of my drink and then looked at Megan. "I'm familiar with literature, Megan. I'm very familiar with lots of literature. In fact, I've been working on a novel myself for the last six months."

There you have it. It just shows you that when you put an exquisitely controlled guy in a foreign environment under the influence of an earthquake, his boss's stare and two vodka tonics, he'd reveal the one secret that he didn't want anyone to know, particularly a woman who had been a central figure at a literary press. As I said, it had occurred that Megan might be a valuable asset when the time was right—forgive me if I'd thought of that angle once or twenty times. I'd heard about her helping one of the ex-Consolidated editors get a short piece published in *The New Yorker*—*The New Yorker!* Megan had given it a cagy editing job, and that woman had quit not long after to go to graduate school in creative writing, buoyed no doubt by Megan's airy hand.

I'd already played out the scenario in my mind how I'd casually drop the info that I'd written a novel around the office, knowing Megan would hear about it. But not now. Not when I was only ten chapters in, and my lead character had become a total asshole when he was supposed to be a hero. Not when I had lost the handle on a story whose handle I had only a loose grip on anyway. So much for playing your cards close to the vest.

And what if the damn latest version was trashed along with my computer?

"A novel! Really? Is the setting contemporary? Let me guess—first person, with a male protagonist. Right?" Her eyes sparkled, and she gave me the first full-blown smile I'd ever seen from her, which freaked me out a little, because she looked cute, and Megan didn't do cute. No.

"Well, yeah, sort of. I mean, he's the protagonist. I mean, the lead guy is the protagonist. Yes. Um, I don't really want to talk about it that much; it's only a little bit done. It's not even close, yet."

God, two drinks and I sound like my brains are tofu. I bent down low over the food and took a couple of big mouthfuls so I wouldn't have to say anything. I didn't have to.

"Of course, the problem with contemporary novels, besides the palpable lack of compelling characterization, is that the reader is often left unfulfilled, served only ambiguity. A kind of veil. There is no true denouement, such as in *Anna Karenina,* or *Madame Bovary.*"

I nodded, visibly chewing. At least I knew the authors of both books, even if I might stumble on a pronunciation. Having a conversation about literature with Megan seemed a little dangerous to me—I'd sampled broadly enough from the menu, but I couldn't really name the full ingredients of any dish. But perhaps I wouldn't be put to any test: liquor may have loosened my tongue, but it seemed to have spurred Megan's to full gallop. She answered all of her own questions and posed others, while she picked up the dishes and moved to the kitchen, talking all the while.

And drinking. She came back from the kitchen with new drinks for us both, without the formality of a freshening inquiry this time.

Considering that Megan had at least done a two-for-one on the drink tally to this point, she had at least four down, and wasn't showing any signs of quenched thirst.

"... and I had to review submissions by first-time authors who had no business writing a grocery list, much less a piece of fiction. Honestly, these are people who wouldn't know a possessive from a predicate. I'm sure your novel at least has its apostrophes in the right places."

She'd been going on for a bit, and I was only half-listening, since I was also trying to hear the earthquake news on the radio, which had been turned down pretty low. Thirty-three confirmed dead so far, and more than that missing. Phone lines useless all over the Bay Area. Damage estimates all over the map. Damn, I hope Sun is all right.

"Yeah, Megan, I'm pretty good with apostrophes. That's why you hired me, right?"

She lifted her glass in a mock toast, drained it, and said, "Right." She gave me a funny look, and then she started rubbing her shoulder. "Hey Hayden. Hey, hey Hayden, how the heck are you?" She giggled and said, "That's not what I mean to say. I meant," and here she leaned forward and said "*meant*" with a jounce of her jaw and a lip-plunging propulsion of the word from her mouth—"to say that my shoulder's been hurting me since I bumped it against a cubicle when one of those quake things hit, excuse me, jolts hit, and it's sore. I want you to look at it—I'll be back in a minute."

She jumped up so quickly it startled me, and half-ran to what I guessed was the bedroom, concealed behind a closed oak door all the while. When she came back, I was more startled than before.

She poured into the room, all flowing and liquidy. I didn't get it at first, but then I saw that the effect was caused by the pants she was wearing, which were un-Meganlike—and then some.

They were a cross between the Arabian nights and Dr. Suess, or at least what I knew of both those subjects. The pants were a pinky, purplish color, and multi-layers, a sort of fluttery, gauzy assemblage of fabric that ballooned from the hips to the ankles, and then tightened with a little elastic cuff. One odd thing was that even though they ballooned just below the hips, they were quite tight right at the hips, revealingly so. But the truly weird thing is that on top she was wearing a sequined purple halter top that had a stringy tie at the back and neck.

That top was very tight, and hard as it was to take my eyes off those pants, that top made it bracingly clear in a way that pin-striped suits never could that Megan was a shapely woman. But that thought was nothing I would have entertained with great enthusiasm, other than the standard hound-dog panting and leg-sniffing of any man. This was Megan, my boss, after all.

But could this harem girl in front of me now be the same Megan? Four vodka tonics told me no. I probably should have mentioned that she brought the half-empty vodka bottle with her, but it was a negligible accessory to her filmy splendor.

I was so flummoxed by the sight of Megan of the Moors that I was speechless. She plopped down alongside me on the couch and turned sidewise, exposing most of her pale, smooth back to me.

"This one," she said, patting her right shoulder. "I bummed it, I bumped it against that cube. Or it bumped me." She laughed again, shaking her head in a way that flipped her hair about her shoulders. It looked like a move you'd see on a shampoo commercial.

I half-turned toward her, but did nothing. I didn't see any kind of bump or bruise on her shoulder, but the light was dim. After a moment, I said, "The right shoulder?" When I said the word "shoulder," my voice went up the ladder a little bit on the second syllable. You'd think I'd never seen my boss, plastered and wearing see-through bloomers before.

"Absolutely, that's the one," she said. "Rub it."

Megan my boss said *rub it,* and rub it I did. At first I just limply squeezed around the top of her shoulder with one hand, but after she'd sort of sighed and settled in, I started working the muscles of her shoulders and neck, trying to make it all better. I'd always thought I could give a gal a nice rub, so rub I did. Megan was amazingly warm, considering the room was now pretty cool; no heater was going to spring to life with the power out.

Megan had poured a good slug of vodka in both our glasses, without any taint of tonic. I'd had a couple of solid swallows, and she'd had a couple more than me. So when she suddenly settled back against my chest when I'd paused in the massage, it was pretty comfy. I was rather warm myself.

She shifted a bit, craned her neck up and toward me and pulled my head to hers and we had one of those warm, slow, sloppy kisses that are a strange, roaming revelation: dizzy, slurping, spiraling.

When we came up for air, I must have looked like a puppy whose food bowl had disappeared in front of him. Megan laughed, and then executed a move that would have given a gymnast a run for her money: she rose up slightly on one arm and spun around so that her legs were encircling my waist on that big couch, and then she drew herself close. She was very warm indeed.

This was the point at which a smarter man would have blurted out a lame excuse, and coughed and sputtered his embarrassed way to the door. But I wasn't a smarter man. I certainly wasn't a sober man. I was a hazy, happy man with a hard-on. And as many surprises as had taken place on this day of quakes and queerness, as the saying goes, I hadn't seen anything yet.

SIX

....

Megan gave a fluttery little laugh, which immediately made me think of a plastered Katherine Hepburn in *The Philadelphia Story* when she's canoodling with a plastered Jimmy Stewart on the night before her wedding. Megan is kind of like Katherine Hepburn in some ways. Here, though, Jimmy never made it to the stage; here we substituted a drunken copyeditor. And Hepburn probably never actually got loop-dee-looped with the help—and never while wearing a come-hither-to-the-Casbah outfit.

Since Megan had flipped a couple of big pillows under and around her, and sort of draped herself under and around them, said harem-girl's outfit had now opened up around the midriff, exposing a band of soft, pale tummy. Sweet tummy, thought the half-blind man. That man was me.

I patted her stomach a bit like you'd pat an agreeable dachshund. That didn't seem right, so I put my palm flat on her warm belly and stroked it a little, watching my hand make its weird path. I didn't want to look at her face, because sozzled as I was, I was still conscious that this was Megan, the Empress of the Day Planner, the woman who silenced the conversation of various minions when she moved past cubicles, the woman who I thought might actually push my novel in front of some gullible, rich publisher. Megan. My *boss.*

Megan, however, had no such qualms. "Hey, Hayden. Hey—Hayden is a lot like hard-on, isn't it? Hayden with a hard-on!" She leaned forward a bit and grabbed the state of my eagerness that had been pointedly pressing against the front of my pants now for a vodka tonic's eternity. I shot my head up and stared at her face, which looked to me a bit like a merry, tipsy elf, or maybe a grinning, fluttery-haired, fluttery-garbed Santa Claus, giving me a gift. But more like Mrs. Claus, because this Santa had breasts.

The breasts. Megan's breasts. But now, now that my cock had made a new friend, I wasn't feeling nearly as formal as the moment before. I felt downright friendly. And thus I leaned forward and put my tummy-patting palm on Megan's right breast, and settled in. She arched her hips and made a whispery little noise, and—all the while keeping a soldier's grip on my business—reached over with her other hand to the floor, where her glass sat with about three fingers of vodka. She drained it, and settled back in to the pillows.

My cue. I maneuvered on top of her small, warm frame and made a vampire's beeline for her neck, while keeping up my unrestrained gropings of her chest. I worked on my repertoire of small bites, lickings and nuzzlings, and Megan settled in to what I thought was a compliant ardor.

Stupor was more like it. I rose up a little off the couch to take a look at my conquest, and found her dead out. "Megan," I said softly. "*Megan,*" I said a bit louder. "Megan, are you awake?" No. But at least she was alive, because I could see that nice tummy and those nice breasts rising and falling with regularity. Cupid's bow had shot some poison darts.

I rose up as the lower parts of me fell, and stood over Megan on the couch, feeling like the conquering hero without his horse. "Megan," I said in a voice I last used as an eleven-year-old. OK. Huh. This hasn't worked out so well. I moved to one of the big picture windows of the room, where I could see a distance down the hill on Taylor. Some of the neighboring apartment buildings had some meager dancing light behind closed curtains—candles. No street-lights at all. A car slowly climbed toward the apartment, the only lights of substance pushing up the hill; I wondered if the driver was thinking about anything but the earthquake.

I was still wearing a couple of coats of vodka, but I was surfacing. Huh, it's not that late; I could probably catch the cable car right on Taylor and hit the Muni on Market to get back down to the Haight. Easy. I walked into Megan's darkened bedroom, where a little re-flection from the big candles showed a broad bed, covered with a large, white quilted bedspread. I brought that back, and settled it softly on Megan. Her mouth was slightly open, and she was breath-ing heavily, though not snoring. Her head was canted weirdly to the side on one of the big pillows, so I gently nudged the pillow so her head was more centered. I was terrified that she would wake up, and think I'd broken into her apartment or something crazy.

But how could what actually happened be any crazier? I blew out all of the candles and inched my way to the door; I stumbled against some big book or box and said "Christ!" aloud, but Megan didn't stir. It was when I was on the third flight of stairs down that I considered it: there's no electricity. There's no cable car, no Muni, no nothing. Shit. OK, I can take a cab. When I made it to street level, I looked back up at the bank of apartments: only a couple had weak, flickery light in their windows; the rest were dark. And the street was quiet, though because of how high on Taylor Megan's apartment was, I could hear some of the usual urban noise. But for most of San Francisco, there was only soft breathing. Punch drunk, like me.

I headed down Taylor, thinking I could catch a cab easily on Columbus. I reached back to pat my wallet in my right rear pocket, and patted only fabric. *My wallet.* I could see it sitting on my desk in my cubicle at work. Or maybe it was *under* my desk after one of those jolts. Or maybe it was buried under the fully collapsed ceiling—who knows what had happened at Consolidated after everything went bonkers? Hayden, you are royally screwed.

I figured I was a four- or five-mile walk back to the lower Haight, maybe back to a house that had no walls. I'm half wasted, I have no wallet, there was a major earthquake in my town and twenty minutes ago I was making moves on a woman who I'd regarded as a cross between Queen Victoria and an adding machine. The prospects for my novel had fallen faster than my puzzled penis. The next person who offered me a vodka tonic would have a contract put out on their life.

SEVEN

....

J acob headed to the Embarcadero up Howard Street thinking he'd like to pass by the little park that overlooks the water, just off of Rincon Point. He'd heard some idiot say the Bay Bridge was down, and he knew that if one thing was true about this quake, it was that the Bay Bridge was still stretching its long steel arms over to the East Bay. Howard turned out to be a mini-Market street: cars askew, people standing wide-eyed or glazedly walking, a couple of emergency-services vehicles with their lights flashing, lots of noise.

Jacob stepped over a man in a suit and tie sitting in the gutter, leaning against a curb. He was gripping both knees with his palms and looking straight ahead, with his briefcase next to him. On the sidewalk behind him, a tipped-over newspaper stand was surrounded by scattered papers, some fluttering in the light wind. Jacob looked back at the man, and at a headline on one of the papers. Something about the World Series.

That's right. Series today, game three! Should have started by now. But the quake. Could a quake stop the World Series? Nah. Jacob stopped and looked back at the businessman lost in thought, as the papers blew around him. *Yeah, this quake might have even stopped the World Series.*

A picture of Sully in his old Giants cap came into his mind. *Damn, Sully might be hurt. Gotta check him out.*

He wheeled and headed back toward Market. Sully worked in front of the Woolworths at the bottom of the old Flood Building near Powell. Jacob grimaced and thought that he might as well check out that stretch of Market and see how the street had actually held up, if he could even tell in the chaos. *Whole street's sorta like my yard, been walking it so long.* He could hear it before he saw it: still lots of sirens and shouts. But when he actually hit Market, it seemed slightly calmer, if you could call *calm* a street teeming with police, blocked vehicles and confused people. And it was getting dark, which gave an odd edge to an already uncomfortable scene.

Broken glass was everywhere, but many of the proprietors of the small liquor stores, delis and discount stores on Market were on their sidewalks, sweeping up. Jacob walked by an old Chevy that had rear-ended a Muni bus; the driver had apparently fled, leaving the driver's side door swinging open. At one point he had to dodge a tall, wild-haired kid who had a big box in his arms, being chased by a cop about twenty steps behind. *Kid must've lifted that from some broken-up storefront. Some days the candy is free.*

Jacob spotted Sully leaning against the entranceway of a disheveled liquor store, just up from the Woolworth's. The big plate-glass window of the store was broken out, but already boarded up. Like many of the small Market Street businesses, the doorway to the store was a big, lockable iron grate that shielded the flimsy wooden doorway from prowlers in the night. A lot of the stores had metal awning-style fences that could be pulled down over the entire storefront at closing time; most of the shadows prowling Market Street at 3am had something extra-legal in mind.

"Sully, my man! You OK?" Sully looked at Jacob and nodded, pulling at his enormous beard. Though Sully was probably still in his thirties, his big beard was liberally laced with grey, as well as with swathes of black, the shade of his slicked-backed hair.

"Oh yeah, doin' fine. Should be dead though. Big piece of masonry came somewhere up top the Flood Building and flying down. Dropped two feet from where I was standing. Woulda killed me for sure." He grabbed at the end of his beard and tugged, so that the end of it coming through his clenched hand looked like a captured rodent. "Saw a guy walk by with his face bleeding like he'd been butchered. Screaming 'Oh God, oh God!'"

He let go of his beard and spat in disgust. "No need to cry out for God now—God ain't never been here, and won't be now. I told you before, but now you know—these are the end times."

Jacob had known Sully for years. He was on Market when Jacob first started begging. You couldn't help but notice Sully: he was at least six-foot-five, and with his beard and flowing hair, made a striking street figure. Like Jacob, he had an established panhandling technique: he leaned against the Woolworth's façade and stuck out his large hand, palm flat. He never said a word. Most people just steered clear of the big outthrust arm, but enough put money in his palm so that coming out for another day made sense. Sully lived in an old shed in a nearby parking lot, where the attendant looked the other way when he went in to sleep.

"Yeah, man. You've told me all about the end times," said Jacob. "You've told me so many times about the end times, that I'm almost ready for the end times, just so I don't have to hear about it any-more."

Sully laughed, head thrown back and body quaking. "S'ok for you, Jacob. God doesn't want your black ass now. He's a little more particular than that." He ran a hand through his greasy hair, and turned to watch a police car, lights flashing but siren off, move slowly down the debris-strewn street. "Actually, I don't think God wants any part of Market Street. Devil neither."

"Listen Sully, you don't happen to know anything about Dexter, do you? I passed by his spot, but didn't see him. Couldn't hear him either."

"No, no Dexter. We might all be better off if that rock had fallen on that horn, with the shit he plays. But I haven't seen him. You're a real mama hen, Jacob. Guess we're all you got. Not much family resemblance, though."

"Not much," said Jacob. Sully knew that Jacob had kids he hadn't seen in a long time; Sully had a boy who was a stranger, a faded face from a workingman's past that seemed like a story told by someone else. Jacob told himself his children's story almost every day, though their faces were fading anyway. Tabby, tall and whippet-thin, maybe even taller now, and Joshua, with his ear-to-ear smile and nervous energy. He tried to keep their stories close, because their bodies were no longer.

Sully pulled a half-pint of vodka from his back pocket, uncapped it and took a long drink. "I'd give you a pull of this brother, but I know it's not your thing any more. More for Sully though, and that's his thing." Across the street, a big shard of glass from an office window above fell to the ground and loudly shattered, sending a shout through the clumps of confused people still crowding Market. Jacob turned rapidly around, face tense. A grey-haired man stood in the middle of the street, looking up. "Was that an aftershock?" he shouted. "Did anyone else feel it?"

Sully took another big drink of vodka. "I feel like I could use another bottle is how I feel. No use trying to gather any more coin today—Market is closed for business." He watched as two very old, very small women, hair close to the same orangish shade, tottered by, clutching each other around the waist. "And I want to be in my shed early tonight, if the sky falls again. Stay safe, Jacob."

Sully picked up the big, faded duffle bag from his side and walked off down Market. Jacob watched his big frame lumber off. He could see the top of the vodka bottle peeking out from Sully's back pocket. *No, no vodka. Not today, and not tomorrow, I hope. I wonder if Tabby would even recognize me. Last time she saw me, at the house in Southern California, I was a falling-down drunk. She wouldn't even look me in the face. Course my face doesn't really turn many heads now either.*

Jacob walked back up Market, toward his alley. It was now dark, the only lights coming from the slowly moving police cars, and a couple of parked emergency vehicles. A few of the upper-story office buildings had a ghostly light, probably from generators. Many of the faces Jacob passed looked distraught. "I heard that the Marina went up like a torch!" a young woman said to her companion as he passed by. "I think we should get out of the City, tonight."

Yeah, get out. But sometimes there's no place to go. Jacob adjusted his backpack on his shoulder, and kept moving slowly up Market.

EIGHT

....

Megan woke up when a beam of morning light struck her across the face. She pushed herself up off the pillows and coughed, and almost gagged. *Uhh, that Chinese food. I should never heat up leftovers.* She swung her legs down to the floor and propped herself up, palms on her knees. *What am I wearing? GOD! Hayden! No!*

She put her head in her hands and plunged her fingers through her hair, over and over. *It's not even possible. A nightmare. Uhh, the earthquake too!* She jumped up, staggered, and moved unsteadily to the wall and flipped a switch. The light from the overhead lamp came through the fluted glass shade with a soft fall. She walked to the telephone and listened to the dial tone. *Power and phone, thank God.*

She looked over at the splayed cushions and pillows of the couch and saw the two glasses on the floor. She shook her head, which hurt, and put the glasses on the coffee table. When she was rearranging the couch cushions, she found Hayden's wallet. *Well, if this isn't my lucky day.* She slapped the wallet down on the coffee table and stood up. *I don't even know what we did. Did I actually have sex with a man I don't even know? Is this what my life is now?*

She took the glasses out to the kitchen, and squinted at the light coming from the high windows and white walls. In the shower, she let the hot water run and run over her neck and back, not moving for ten or fifteen minutes. *Can the building even be open? It's probably just superficial damage. Perhaps I can even get a little work done if no one's around. The Essex contract is incomplete. Wait, my day planner! I left it at the office!*

She snapped the faucet handles shut and flung the shower curtain back, her face a mask of frustration. When she stepped to her bedroom, she thought she could hear the clanking of a cable car. *Are there ever earthquakes the day after an earthquake? No matter. I'm going.* She dressed hurriedly and headed downstairs, but not before putting Hayden's wallet in her purse.

In the foyer of the apartment building she saw several cardboard boxes filled with broken glass and porcelain objects, probably dishware or perhaps decorative figurines. *I suppose I'm lucky on one count.* She was reaching for the large, mottled brass knob on the building's entrance door when the door swung open from the outside. Megan drew back, involuntarily throwing her arm over her chest. *Mr. Turknot, drat!*

"Megan, yes! Megan, isn't it? Remember me, Tuttle? Good morning to you! Quite a shaker we had yesterday, wasn't it? Not something I had much truck with in Iowa."

Turknot was wearing a kind of hunter's cap, with of all things, a plume, perhaps from an ostrich. Megan, startled, stared at his hat for a moment before she replied. "Yes, Mr. Turknot, that was a real earthquake. My first one. I hope it's my last. Is your apartment all right?"

Turknot tugged at the brim of his cap, making the plume bounce. "No real problems. I have a tropical fish tank, 30 gallons, that sloshed onto the floor a bit, but it's in a heavy frame that's bolted to the wall—I read all about these California quakes, and I was ready! How did your garden do up there?"

My garden! The roses! Megan thought about going back upstairs, but decided against it. "Thank you for asking, Mr. Turknot. In all the excitement, I didn't get a chance to survey the garden. I'm sure it's fine. And now I've got to get to work."

"Work? Oh Megan, the power is back on and all, and the Muni is up, but I don't think many businesses are going to be up and running today. I've just been for a long walk through the business districts, and many of the buildings are shuttered. Some even had guards in front."

As he talked, Megan looked both at the bobbing plume and the bobbing of Turknot's prominent Adam's apple. She focused back on his face. "I appreciate your concern, Mr. Turknot, but I have a lot of responsibilities, and I need to at least stop by the office. Goodbye."

"Well, good luck. Be careful." He walked around her and started upstairs, but turned on the first step. "But it's Tuttle, Megan. Tuttle. No need to call me Mr. Turknot."

"Very well, Mr. Tur—er, Tuttle. Take care."

Where could he have come across that hat? Goodness. Though it took longer than usual, she was able to catch a cable car down to Market, and then the Muni that stopped close to the Consolidated building. Most of the conversations on the cars were about the collapsed section of freeway in Oakland that had crushed many cars and their inhabitants. The death toll was unclear, but two people on the Muni were arguing about whether the body count would be in the hundreds when they cleared the rubble. Megan tried not to listen.

There was a great deal of debris on Market, with some street dumpsters filled with splintered wood, torn metal and big shards of glass. She had seen what looked like uniformed guards or police officers in front of a few of the larger office buildings. There weren't any guards in front of Consolidated, but she could see a large sign on the door when she walked up. It read: "Building closed until further notice. Safety inspection will begin today." There was a number to call for further information.

Megan stamped her foot, and flattened her lips. *I need that day planner.* She had a key to the office, but not to the building. She'd actually discussed it with Mr. McManus the other day, saying it would help when she wanted to catch up on some projects. He said he'd check into it. Of course he would—they always like to know that the executive team is willing to come in on the odd weekend or two.

She started to write down the number and then stopped. *They won't know anything.* She snapped the pad and pen back into her purse and began walking back up to the Muni stop. When she passed by a long alley between building fronts she heard some shouting. A little distance into the alley, she saw two men standing over a man on the ground, who was holding his hand over his face. There was a lot of shouting that she couldn't understand, but she recognized that the man lying on the ground was the disabled man who begged in front of Consolidated, the one with the prosthetic leg. She stared as the shorter of the two standing men kicked the disabled man in the chest.

Megan looked around for someone to help. No police in sight. A smartly dressed businesswoman walked quickly by with clicking high heels. There was a coffee stand about a quarter of a block away with a man out front. Megan started to shout, but then turned back to the alley when she heard someone groan. The shorter man had pulled a big leather bag or pouch away from the man on the ground, and both standing men were looking into it.

Megan took two steps into the alley. "Get away from him! I've called the police! Leave that man alone!"

The taller of the two, a skinny black man in his twenties, stepped toward Megan. "Well, look at this shit. One-legged nigger has a fine white woman to protect him. I need to get me one of those." He was holding what appeared to be a table leg or squared-off club in one of his hands, and he waved it in the air.

Megan stepped back almost to the sidewalk. "I told you, I've called the police. They will be here any time!" Her voice slipped on the "any," rising in register so that the last word came out almost as a squeak. Both of the men were facing her now, and she could see that the short one was very raggedly dressed. He was possibly Hispanic, maybe Italian, and could have been under eighteen. He turned to his companion and said, "Fuck this noise, and fuck that bitch. Let's book." Both of them turned away and moved in the other direction, out of the alley at a trot.

Megan watched as the disabled man pushed himself up to a sitting position, and leaned against the wall. She noticed he wasn't wearing his prosthetic, and she grimaced when she saw it off to the side, leaning against some kind of cabinet against the opposite wall that had its door open. The man wasn't looking at her. She turned to walk back up Market, paused, then turned back to the alley, and began walking up to the disabled man.

"Excuse me, I'm sorry, are you hurt?" Megan walked to within 10 feet of the man and stopped. She could see that he had a large lump on his forehead, which he was rubbing with his hand. She held her head back, expecting him to exude a foul smell.

The man waved his hand at Megan. "Ehh, I'm not hurt. Take more than a couple of pokes from those punk-ass punks to hurt me. They took my cash bag though." He looked up at Megan, and his eyes narrowed and he gave a quick nod. "Probably a week's wages. And a Bronze Star and a Purple Heart." He shrugged. "Those aren't worth that much, though."

"Well, I'll help you to notify the police and perhaps they can get your star and heart back. Were those awards of some kind? And your bag as well." She could see inside the cabinet, which seemed to be an electrical power box of some sort. There was room for a fairly big duffel bag that was compressed into the corner. She could see a toothbrush and what looked like a folded pocketknife on the cabinet floor. There was a makeshift roof of cardboard over the ground that used the top of the cabinet for a support; an old sleeping bag was unfolded underneath.

The man pushed himself to his feet, and hop-stepped over to his artificial leg. Megan stepped back. He quickly snapped the leg into place and turned to Megan. "No, you know, a Bronze Star. Oh, never mind. And no, no police! Police won't do a cussed thing. I'll find those punks in due time. I do thank you for your concern."

That leg. Oh. "Well, my name is Megan Thornstock, and I work in this building at Consolidated Leasing," she said, pointing to the offices above. If you need any help identifying those criminals, you can find me there." She started to step away, when she saw the back of a torn-up novel against the wall where he fell. Its pages were scattered around the alley, but she could see the back cover. *Wuthering Heights.* She took a step toward the disabled man.

"Sorry, but are you reading that? I mean, is that novel yours?"

"Well, yeah, what's left of it. Was already missing a section, but those stupid kids grabbed it and tore it up. I was only two-thirds through. Maybe I can look at it in the library though."

Megan smiled. "You mean you are interested in the Brontes? You know that that work, *Wuthering Heights,* was Emily's only novel? Though in some ways it's considered better than Charlotte's *Jane Eyre,* which is an epic, as far I'm concerned. Not that *Heights* isn't epic as well."

Jacob took off his glasses and rubbed his nose. The bump on his head was starting to discolor, a soft bluish shade on his dark skin. "Well, this is my first Bronte. I didn't know there was a whole family of them." He stepped forward toward Megan and put out his hand. "Jacob Reed. I do *know* you, though. I've seen you outside the building many times."

Megan shook his hand, surprised that his fingernails were clean. Jacob had put an emphasis on the word "know" that puzzled Megan. She nodded at him and said, "Well, good day, Mr. Reed. I do hope you recover your belongings." She walked away, but when she reached the head of the alley, she turned back and looked at Jacob. He was leaning against the alley wall, rubbing his chin. *Wuthering Heights. You just never know.*

She looked in her purse for Muni fare, and saw Hayden's wallet. *Oh, damn. I really should call Hayden as soon as possible. But his number is in my employee log, in my planner. Maybe he's listed.* She made her way to the Muni stop, noting how few people were on the street. *Well, an earthquake certainly makes walking on Market easier.*

NINE

··

Took me a couple of hours, maybe more, to hit the Lower Haight, where I hang my hat. I'm used to walking in the City, with its whooping ups and drooping downs, but after wringing an earthquake, a few vodkas and an indescribable experience with my boss through my system, I was beat. The walk home had been weirdly quiet; there are a lot of nighttime wanderers out in the City at any given hour, but I only saw a few pedestrians, a couple of small groups around trashcan fires, New York–style, and some lanterns or candles flickering in windows. Oh, and a broken water line. Basically, *All Quiet on the Shattered Front*.

Except for my block. My block is Pierce, and my house is a few houses up from Page. This is not exactly Park Place. My block has the distinction of not one, but two crack houses on it, and if you know anything about those jumpy little rocks, you know they don't induce Zen meditation. My street always has jangled night nerves, people amped, wanting stuff and getting it, wanting more, and getting angry when anything—like a 30-second delay—interfered with the getting.

I sleep—if you want to call it that—on the street-side of the block, and since I'm not the most accomplished sleeper anyway, I'm often twisted from my bed by some forlorn cry or buzzing curse or wracking cough. Or something or somebody being smashed. It's no phenomenon to me now, but when I first moved in, I was amazed that whenever I went to my window in the middle of the night, two-thirty, three-thirty, four-thirty, I'd always see somebody wandering about, or clusters of somebodies buzzing like flies, usually around the two doorways of the happy houses. The crack dispensaries were on opposite ends of the block, on the other side of the street from my house, so that I could scan from my facing window and easily see the party that never ends.

One night I heard an argument and looked out and saw a young white guy and a peroxide-blonde black woman bickering, and within seconds he gave her a hard right to the face and I could hear, sickeningly, her teeth or her jaw break. That one, I called the cops. Most of the time I'd just look out, see the spiders crawling around, and then go back to bed with a pillow over my head.

Tonight, though, mostly quiet. Couple of loungers lounging outside the crack emporium on the high side of the street. I'd always enjoyed their porch light, which was totally film noir: a twenty-five-watt bulb, so that all the business was conducted in a ghostly glow. I checked the Studey, which was parked conveniently-but-illegally, wrapped around the corner curb on Page, to see if anyone had busted one of the windows looking for all the diamond brooches I kept in the glove box. I'd learned pretty quickly down here that you don't leave a damn thing—and I mean not even sandwich wrappers—on your seats or dash, or some pipehead is going to crawl into your car after it. The Studey was sound.

My house looked intact from the outside. It's a Victorian, built a bit after the turn of the century. It's not one of the real fancy ones, and hasn't been painted outside in years, but it's got nice bay windows, gables and small columns. The big iron-barred gate I have to open before I get to the actual door isn't quite turn-of-the-century. More like turn of the crackpipe, or to turn the pipe users aside. Our house is actually two flats, as are many of the neighborhood houses, which are big enough to have multi-bedroom home spaces on separate floors. There are three bedrooms in my flat. My bedroom, Roland's—who never comes out of his room, so his room is his house—and Drew's.

Drew is the tenant who's been there the longest, and in many ways, though I'd been there going on two years, it still seemed like it was his house. Most of the furniture and kitchenware was his, and he'd spent some time painting the interior, which was a crazy mélange of brightly colored walls that shouted when the sun streamed in through the tall windows.

Drew was drinking tea in the kitchen when I came in.

"Hey, hey, Dorothy comes home from the tornado! Where's Toto?" said Drew.

I laughed. I looked around the house in a sweeping pan, and couldn't see anything amiss. There were no lights, of course, but

Drew often lit candles anyway, and he had a full army of flaming soldiers lit in the kitchen and the big living room.

"I think Toto's getting interviewed on Channel Five," I said. "So, you survived. How about the house? And is Roland OK?"

Drew waved a thin arm and smiled. "House sailed through. I think we're on bedrock out here. One casualty: the biggest gazing ball fell off the table and shattered. No great loss. Anyway, that gives me an excuse to go shopping."

The apartment had lots of little "touches," like the small-to-big series of silver-mirrored glass balls on the big glass coffee table in the living room. One less was fine with me. More room for my big feet, though I didn't put them up on the table when Drew was around. It's strange: Drew is a couple of years younger than me, but in some ways he's like a big brother. And sometimes even like a father.

Of course, that's excepting the times when he's a crazy person, which is also one of his roles. He's a bartender in the Castro, and also puts together big, showy flower arrangements there a few times a week, and in a couple of other Castro bars. That means that he gets up around 3am twice a week to go get these exotic flowers from the Flower Mart, because they open at 2, and he's got to get the good stuff.

He took a sip of tea. "Roland's fine. As you might imagine, he was in his room. I was at the bar, which lost a bunch of glasses, but no big deal. They closed and I came home. Roland and I had a regular conversation, which was refreshing. Then he went back in his room."

Drew ran his hand through his cropped blond hair. He wore his hair in a crew cut, the look I had when I was seven, though it looked a little better on Drew. His hair color wasn't what God gifted him with, but Drew wasn't expecting much from God anyway. So yeah—Drew works in the Castro, arranges flowers, and dyes his hair blond. He laughs at his own gay stereotype. Though he's not really a fluttery type, I thought he might be gay when he first interviewed me about living in the house.

When he'd told me on the phone later that he thought I was the best candidate, I had about a half-hour's hesitation—because I'm such a manly man and all—but I liked him right off the bat, and thought what the hell. Now he's one of the people I feel the most at ease with in the whole city. But man, does he have some lulus for friends. And I'll get to some of his parties later.

He coughed loudly and said, "I'm so used to being up at this time of night that I can't sleep. I listened to the radio for a while. The Marina was hit hard, with big fires. And did you hear about that Oakland freeway? I feel so bad for those people and their families." He cleared his throat and said, "Maybe God finally did lay the hammer down on Sodom and Gomorrah. I have a feeling that sodomy will remain popular though." He laughed and coughed again.

"Very funny, funny guy. Hey, you should do something about that cough. It seems like you've been coughing for a couple of weeks. Anyway, I'm heading for bed. This has been a day to remember or a day to forget. I'll tell you which one in the morning."

I started to head to my bedroom, and then I veered to the phone. Same baap-baap-baap-baap as before. "Hey, did you hear anything on the news about Santa Cruz? I'm hoping my old digs don't have to be dug out."

Drew looked up. "Actually, I did hear something about Santa Cruz. The epicenter of the quake was down there somewhere. Last I heard they'd revised it up from 6.9 to 7.0, but it's still preliminary. A few people did die down in Santa Cruz County too, but I'm not sure on the details."

Shit. The epicenter. Shit. "Wow. Thanks man. I'm hitting it. I'll see you tomorrow."

I went into my room and lay down on the bed without undressing. I kept seeing Sun and the loony way she used to dance around the house, sometimes even without music, her long, dark hair whirling. That house was old and funky, way funkier than our place on Pierce. I got undressed and into bed, putting in the earplugs right off the bat. No crackhead yelp was going to penetrate tonight.

I drifted off to sleep thinking of my hand under Megan's top and then trying not to think of my hand there. Either way, I lost.

#######

I woke up late morning, windows streaming sun. When I headed to the bathroom, I noticed its light and several other lights were on in the house. Drew must have flicked the switches on some lights and left them up when the power went out. Drew's door was open, and I peeked in, but he was gone. Could the bar be open in the Castro? Roland's door was shut as usual, and that was message enough for me.

I picked up the phone in the kitchen. Normal dial tone. I put it back. I wasn't hungry for breakfast, so I sat at the table for a bit. Then I picked up the phone and dialed. She was home.

"Sun, hey, it's Hayden, gosh are you all right?"

"Hey Hay-den." She always stretched out my name, even when she was angry with me. Hay-den. I never told her how much I loved it. Her parents were from some Podunk town in Iowa, but she had a drawling way of talking, southernish, with a little smile behind those ripe lips. "Yeah, we're OK. One broken window. But downtown is trashed. Two people died, and I think someone else in Watsonville. I was at the yoga center doing a class and a big shelf came crashing down with all this stuff on it. One of the doors was damaged. Everybody ran out."

We're OK. Right. Her and Total Loser Surfer Boyfriend. Like that's a "we're." He'd moved in three weeks after I left. She tried to tell me that they were just friends at first, but I'd heard how friendly they were. Just one of those last-straw things anyway. In my head back then, I'd been gone for months.

"Well, listen, I'm really glad you're OK. Did you try to call here?"

The pause was long. "No, but I thought about it. Are you OK?"

"Yeah. The office rolled around like it was in the ocean. Lots of broken computers and equipment. Nobody died there though, but I'm sure you've heard about all the other deaths and the fires. The City is trashed. At least the electricity's on."

"Well, that's really good Hay-den. It's nice to hear your voice too. I'm glad you're safe." There was a pause. "Well, take care."

"Sun, Sun, wait—listen, I need to talk to you about something. Not a big deal, but I'd like to talk to you. I need to return a bunch of CDs to Will anyway, and I've been promising him for a while. With the way the office looked, I don't think it will be open for the next couple of days. Could I just make it down tomorrow afternoon and come over?"

I could see her, I could hear her looking off, in that placid, dreamy way, debating whether to say no, or on a whim, say yes. She was never able to explain to me how she made decisions. She just made them.

"OK Hay-den, that's fine. Maybe around one. But I promised to come to the center and help clean up later in the day, so we can only talk for a bit."

So what if there were no CDs? So what if I didn't have a clue what I wanted to talk to her about? I hadn't seen her in almost a year, and then for only twenty minutes while I was down visiting Will. Maybe her A-hole mellow-head surfer buddy won't be around. Maybe it'll be like old times. Maybe I should just shut up, but it would be nice to get out of the City.

TEN

....

Jacob sat against the alley wall, staring at the scattered pages of the novel. He absently rubbed his head where the kid had clapped him with his club. *Getting real old,* he thought. *Never coulda crept up on me like that in country. Would have taken them both out, two shots. Hell, old.*

He walked over to the electrical enclosure box on the alley wall and pulled out the duffel. He'd relied on just turning the hasp of the broken lock to make it look like it was still locked, but he knew he'd have to get his own lock for it now. *But what if the electric company comes and needs to check the box, with my lock on it? Damn.*

He dug deep into the duffel and pulled out a worn metal tub, with a close-fitting lid. Inside was a clump of bills, a scattering of twenties, tens, fives and ones. This was his "safety money," what he kept aside from the money bag, in case the money bag was lost or stolen. The safety money added up to a little under two hundred dollars, though he hadn't counted it in a long time. It also held his bankbook.

Today's deposit is going to be a little shy. But I don't want to be carrying much of this, or leaving it without the lock, if this is how my luck is going. He stuffed the duffel back in the box, turned the broken lock, and walked up the alley toward Market. When he hit Market, he turned and began walking down the street, past Consolidated's building. Megan's face came into his mind.

She's a drinker. That's it! That's why she seems familiar. Drink knows drink. He'd seen her many times enter the building in the mornings, eyes red-rimmed, nose damp. But it hadn't been clear to him until he'd seen her up close, talking of Bronte. *Spouting. But with all the confidence, still that certain haze. Wonder how bad she's got it? Well, not my problem.*

The bank had a big line of duct tape diagonally across one of the tall plate-glass windows, but it was open. He gave way to someone behind him in line in order to wait for his favorite teller, Patricia, the young redheaded girl who must drink enough coffee in the morning to make her blood boil, by the perky way she treated everyone. He'd been banking there for years, and she'd been there for at least two, and she'd never batted an eye at his worn clothes or unkempt appearance. She knew he was on the streets.

"Mr. Reed! Very nice to see you again! But what's that on your forehead? Did something fall on you during the earthquake?" She smiled a thousand watts, and pulled his deposit slip and his envelope in front of her.

"Nope, I ducked. Just like Chicken Little. Had some trouble with some punks, but it's fine."

"Oh Mr. Reed. I really wish you wouldn't keep risking it. You do have the means to stay inside, you know. And there's also the disability payments—were you to apply, you'd certainly qualify." She entered some numbers into the computer and looked back at Jacob.

He shook his head and pursed his lips. "No disability. Government put me in that war. I won't take anything from the government. And I don't need to live inside." He nodded slowly at her, with a slight smile.

She frowned slightly, then brightened again. "It's very, very, very good that you came in today, very good! Your wife, well, your ex-wife called. She said she's your ex-wife. She's very upset about not being able to get in touch with your daughter down in Santa Cruz. I didn't know you had a daughter!"

Jacob drew back, and pulled at the front of his shirt. "My wife? But how'd she know?" He wiped his hand across his jaw. "Oh, no, right—I told her about the bank, in case anything happened. My daughter, yes, Tabitha. She's nineteen." He smiled, then frowned. "Smart as a whip. But what's this about Santa Cruz?"

Patricia printed out the deposit statement and handed it to Jacob. "Well, I'm sure you needn't be worried, but I heard that Santa Cruz had a lot of damage, and I guess your wife had tried to get in touch with your daughter many times, but couldn't. She left this number for you to call her."

The teller handed him another piece of paper with a name and phone number on it. Janisha Reed. *Still with the Mobile area code, so still living in her mama's house. Janisha Reed. Name doesn't even sound right any more.*

He had been standing there staring at the paper for a minute, when the teller tried to whisper to him, but succeeded in speaking in a kind of sibilant yell. "I'm sorry Mr. Reed, but there's another customer behind you. I hope everything works out!" Her smile could have picked a lock.

Jacob nodded and walked slowly out of the bank, looking at the scribbled name and number. Could Tabby actually be hurt? He'd glanced over a front-page quake article in the *Chronicle* at a news-stand, and had seen that Santa Cruz was the quake's origin. She's got to be fine. But what if she isn't?

Jacob was the one who wanted to name his daughter Tabitha, and he'd overruled his wife, even though he was still overseas. He'd named her after the daughter of a character on a 60s sit-com, "Be-witched," knowing all along that it was just another stupid comedy about white people in the suburbs. But he couldn't deny his crush on the lead actress, Elizabeth Montgomery, who played a witch. Jacob felt a strange sympathy for witches.

Damn, having to call Janisha! It must be two years. I can still hear the stink of her last words. "Are you sure you haven't taken a drink since then? Maybe you've had a few and don't even remember. Most days you didn't remember shit." *No, I remember lots of shit. It was all shit at the end. I wish I could forget.*

He stuck the note in his pocket and headed up Market to a phone booth.

ELEVEN

M egan returned to her apartment in the late morning.
She had walked all the way down Market to 7th, turning around before she hit 6th Street, which had such
a profusion of derelicts, prostitutes and wild-eyed men, young and
old, that she avoided it. Sixth always left her shaken, forced to consider the state of the San Francisco streets. Not that the rest of
Market was greatly different—Sixth Street just seemed to be a con-
densed version.

She took the walk because she'd hoped that when she went back
by Consolidated the office would be open. But nothing had
changed. What had changed from yesterday was that the streets
were much quieter. But still a tremendous mess, with a lot of trucks
in front of various buildings, including many vehicles with city in-
signias. Many office buildings had red tape across their entrances
preventing access, and a few still had what appeared to be security
personnel in front. There were also more police cars than usual,
some parked in the transit lanes, though the Muni was running.

But again, no entrance into Consolidated, and thus no day planner and thus no work. Except perhaps some cleaning up of her
apartment. Back home, she lit a cigarette and sat in the big leather
armchair that faced the living room windows. After she finished

smoking the first, she lit another. There was a big crash outside her apartment that she immediately thought was an aftershock, and she leaped to her feet and headed to the door, dropping the lit cigarette on the floor. Just someone dropping something big in the hall. *Goodness, my nerves.* She stubbed the cigarette out in an ashtray.

Her chest tightened, and her stomach rolled slightly. *No. Not before lunch. I'll just have some water.* She slipped her cigarettes back into her purse and saw Hayden's wallet. *Drat!* There wasn't much in there: a driver's license showing a Hayden with very short hair, a credit card, a gas-station credit card, a couple of receipts, a loyalty card from a local Thai restaurant and a photo of Hayden and a pretty, dark young woman with long hair. The photo looked like it might have been posed, because Hayden was sitting in profile to the young woman, looking very stern. Megan looked at the photo for a moment, and then started putting everything back. She noticed that the back of the restaurant card had a Pierce Street address written on it, along with a phone number. *Hmm. Hayden told me that he lived on Pierce Street. Could that be his number?*

She walked to the phone and as she was about to pick it up, it rang. "Ms. Thornstock? This is Elsa Quicken from the university at Santa Cruz. I'm sorry to call you at home, but you'd given me your home number, and when I called at your office today, there was no answer."

"Elsa, yes, nice to hear from you. The office is closed today; they are assessing the damage, though I don't believe it was severe. How can I help you?" Megan sat on the edge of the telephone chair, tugging at the ends of a hank of hair.

"Well, I don't want to be the bearer of bad news after you've experienced such a shock, but I think that the University will have to cancel the contract for the electronic equipment. The budgetary problems are more severe than expected, and we can't carry a contract of that magnitude. In fact, the computer lab itself may not even be completed."

Megan felt the discomfort in her stomach again. She looked up at the kitchen door, and then settled back into the chair. "Elsa, Consolidated is a company with many resources and a good deal of flexibility. We could potentially offer to underwrite the lease ourselves, and we can certainly consider a renegotiation of terms. I'm sure you don't want to deny the students the kind of advantages this equipment would provide."

There was a pause on the other end of the line. "Well, you're right about the students. But we have to operate under the budget's constraints. And there might be legal issues regarding re-sourcing any loans. I'm going to have to speak to some of the other officers of the university's budget office and get back to you."

This would be the second lease of Megan's, one of two that she had personally overseen, that would have fallen apart within the last two months. Not going to happen. "Elsa, I'd like to come down to the office in the next day or so and discuss this with you and your colleagues. We'd like to reach out to you and work this out."

"Yes, that's possible. I'll get back to you by tomorrow at the latest. I do hope we can work something out."

After hanging up, Megan walked quickly into the kitchen, opened the liquor cabinet and pulled out a bottle of vodka. She went to the refrigerator and looked up at the clock. Twelve-seven. *Perfect.* She pulled out a bottle of tonic water and fixed a drink. She was two-thirds of the way through her second when she remembered that she wanted to call Hayden.

"Hayden, is that you? It's Megan, Megan Thornstock. Do you have a moment?" She walked the phone over to the big couch, wrapping its long cord around her wrist.

"Uh, yeah, yes Megan, it's me. How are you? Are you OK?"

"Of course I'm OK. You mean from last night?" She laughed slightly, and it came out in a stuttering yip, like a small dog's cry. "I do apologize for the drinking. I'd never been in an earthquake, and I was shaken up. Literally." She laughed again in the same skittering way, and then abruptly cut off the laughter. "Hayden, I have no real excuse for what took place between us, but it was an errant incident, and a private matter, and I am trusting in your discretion." She finished her drink and held up the empty glass to the light.

"That's fine, Megan. I mean, I understand. I had a few drinks too and didn't mean for us to go overboard. I mean it was fun, but—I mean, I understand about the discretion."

"Fine. We don't need to discuss that again; I think the foremost thing to remember is that I am your supervisor. I do consider us to be friends, but our office relationship is paramount." She paused for a moment, and when Hayden didn't answer, she continued. "The reason I called is that I have your wallet, which you left here. I'm uncertain when the office is opening again, so I wanted you to know that I could have it brought to you if you like." Megan stretched her legs on the couch, and shook the glass a little so that the ice cubes tinkled.

"The wallet, yes! I *do* need my wallet. I have to drive to Santa Cruz tomorrow or the next day, and I need my license. Can I come and get it, or what?"

Megan sat up on the couch. "Santa Cruz? Really? One of our important contracts with the university is in distress, and I need to go there too. I was going to rent a car, but I am an uncertain driver, and I've never even been to Santa Cruz. Could I possibly go with you?"

Hayden waited a moment before speaking. "Well, sure, uh, I could probably drive you down. I'm going to see my old, my old friend there in the mid-afternoon, and I'm not certain when I'm going back up. So I guess I could drop you off at the U. and then come back and get you or something."

Megan sat up and made a note on the pad she kept on the coffee table. "That sounds as though it could work, Hayden. I will probably need between two and three hours at the university, perhaps even more, because I may need to speak to a committee as well as our contact there. Why don't you be here at ten tomorrow morning and we'll leave immediately from there?"

"Ten? Well, yeah. I actually hadn't made up my mind that I was going tomorrow, but if it can make something work out for you at Consolidated, I can probably work with that. I'll give you a call later this evening if there's a problem."

Megan hung up, and leaned back on the couch with a smile. She looked at the frieze of figures and artwork that bordered the high ceiling of the room, fixing on an ornate working of a rose just beginning to open. *The roses.* She rose quickly and walked to and through the terrace door and up the rooftop's staircase. One look told her more than she wanted to know.

The quake had knocked the arbor completely to the ground, breaking the two main support poles. Worse off were the roses. Whatever building twist had tossed the arbor had also wrenched the rose trunks almost completely out of the soil. Most of the bigger canes were broken or cracked. Some of the other flowers in the base of her bed were fine, but the roses looked like they might be a total loss.

Megan sat on the chair and looked at the roses for a couple of minutes. *This was really all I had to show Father. I wasn't even certain if they would ever come, but I would have the roses to show him if they did. I'd show him I still had a hand in, had something of substance going. Besides the job, which he wouldn't care about if I were the mayor of San Francisco. Now there's nothing.*

She put her father's image out of her mind and went back downstairs to her apartment. She decided to start rearranging the books after she'd had another drink. *It makes much more sense to sort the works by publication chronology rather than author name. Then I can consider how one influenced the other, and the flow of stylistic developments.* She began pulling the large volumes off the shelves, occasionally hugging one to her chest.

TWELVE

··

I woke up thinking about my novel. Of course, if I was actually working on my novel, rather than thinking about it, I might have more than ten little chapters. It really isn't that bad of an idea for a novel, but I suppose that's like saying, "This cottage cheese doesn't smell that bad; it's probably OK to eat." The more I thought about it, my novel was even more like that bad cottage cheese, because it had been sitting around for several months without anyone poking a spoon into it.

I really don't just leave stuff hanging, or abandon something just because it isn't easy. I think the problem is that I care too much about the novel. It's sort of my fantasy ticket, where I jettison my life of mediocrity and do something of substance. Sure, I sort of included the slaps on the back from the literati and maybe seducing a babe correspondent from *The New Yorker* who came by to interview me on my stunning debut, but really, at the base level, I wanted to touch people with an insightful piece of literature. Or at least some good writing, literary or not. I can say that without smirking. On good days.

Here's the deal: I wanted to do a family dynamic kind of epic, based loosely on *The Brothers Karamazov,* but contemporary. Mix it up a bit: the dad's a media mogul, crusty, controlling dude, his two sons are two years apart, one a big head-butting rival to his dad like Dimitri, the other kind of a saintly type like Alyosha, but by way of Hesse's *Siddhartha* character, kind of a philosopher ninja. And instead of a third son, there's a daughter, the intellectual parallel to Ivan, but she's got a bad coke habit. And instead of the dad getting murdered, he gets kidnapped. And of course it looks like the kids are involved.

So, I'm thinking the genre is a literary thriller. It moves through the first chapters, developing character and plot, with some explosive family tangles. And I get the dad kidnapped and set up the "who did it?" among the family members and the ransom biz with the cops. And then I stalled. Like dead-stalled. I could kill the dad like in *Karamozov,* but I thought that instead I could build family tension from the inside, have tension with the police from the outside, and then introduce a mystery element.

But my mystery element has continued to be a mystery, to me and all concerned. I never was that good at outlining stories—I was sure if I winged this one, it would take wing. But so far it's more of an emu than an eagle. I read the whole thing over this morning. It stunk. If fact, it seemed to literally stink. I could have sworn I smelled something like old cheese coming from the pages. What's worse, the truly latest version, with a chapter I didn't have at home, was on the computer at work.

To this point, I'd had two short stories published: one in a small literary journal, and one in the college literary magazine. Faulkner was trembling in his grave. But maybe I was on to something with my novel—literature that might be unreadable, but you could eat it. That was the savory thought I had when Megan rang the bell.

I let her in through the outside gate and she came a few steps up the stairs. She was wearing a formless beige jacket with a long-ish beige skirt. She didn't quite blend in with our Fauvist walls. "Well, Hayden, this is certainly colorful," she said, looking every-where but at me. "I haven't been in all that many homes here, but this one would really stand out if it were in Boston. And your neighborhood is pretty colorful too."

"Right. My roommate, uh, my housemate is the man with the artist's touch," I said, looking over her head. "I can't claim respon-sibility for the neighborhood either. Do you want to come up to check it out?"

"Perhaps we should just go, though I would enjoy seeing the rest of the house." She glanced at her watch and looked up, fixing her eyes on my chest. So, this was how it was going to work: Megan and I would take two hours to drive to Santa Cruz, and never look at one another. Maybe I could spend the rest of my career at Con-solidated looking at Megan's shoulder while she looked at mine when we encountered one another. Works for me, I suppose.

I had been struggling to keep the image of her in that halter-top and those diaphanous bloomers out of my head, but it emerged with a vengeance. Ahh, vodka. The person who invented it could never have foreseen Megan in that outfit. That was more colorful than any of my walls.

I pointed to the gate and we both went out. To the left out in front of the house was a giant stack of garbage and other items: a keeled-over shelf, a big old television without a cord, something that might have been an industrial hair dryer or maybe a grinding tool, assorted clothes. Megan might have presumed that the pile was earthquake leavings, but that was what our sidewalk looked like on any day. The interesting thing was that those objects might all be gone by late afternoon, and replaced with equally fascinating ones the next morning. But if Megan presumed anything, she spoke not.

I pointed to the Studey, which was wrapped around the curb of the corner opposite the house. She pointed at it as well. "That?"

"That," I said.

I shouldn't have let it bug me. I mean, people who don't dig old cars just don't get it. Studebaker had a storied history of true auto oddity, making a series of space-age models in the early 60s, one of which was notable for casual observers not being able to tell the front end from the rear end. Sure, my Lark wasn't one of the real collectibles, but for being 25 years old, it was clean, cherry even. Of course, many mornings it preferred to stay clean and stationary, since its engine could be a bit balky.

But it started right up. I headed out of town toward 280 by way of 19th, thinking I'd cut over at Half Moon Bay and cruise the coast, since it was a sparkler of a day. Nobody spoke. As we headed through the Sunset District, I pointed out a couple of houses where there were some fallen chimneys or large piles of debris. Megan looked up and said, "Mmm," but that's it.

But I don't like a pot unstirred. "So, contract problems, huh? I didn't even know we had a contract at UCSC. You're kind of like Mister Fixit Man, riding in to save the day?" I turned my head to look at her, but she was staring face-forward, clutching her purse on her lap, as she had been from the moment we'd left. "I guess that's more like Ms. Fixit Woman, though, a bit more—"

"Hayden, as with any company of size, there are often extenuations and adjustments in the contract structures. You are aware that contracts and their negotiations are part of what I do at Consolidated; face-to-face consultations are just part of the process."

I glanced over when she finished, and saw her flip her hair up over her shoulder, the same way she'd done it the other night at her apartment. But her shoulder was bare then. I tried to think of something to say that would jokingly refer to that night, but kind of minimize it. But then I thought of how stupid that would be. And then I did it anyway.

"So, Megan, the other night, I know it got a little weird—"

The blue, blue of her eyes. Piercing, really, cliché or not. And I mean really piercing, because she hadn't responded, but was simply staring at me, across the gold-and-tan plaid pattern of my Studebaker's seat, which matched her outfit quite well. But her attitude now: not beige.

"Hayden, I discussed that with you on the phone. I needn't elaborate again, but just so the matter is settled: The earthquake frightened me. I'd taken a sedative when we arrived at the house, and I probably had one drink too many."

My glance moved from Megan to the road and back. She held her head with her chin jutting slightly up and when she finished speaking, her lips flatlined.

"Furthermore, the contact that took place between us was an unfortunate accident, and I apologize for my part in it. I'm hoping we can resume the friendly, professional relationship that we've always enjoyed."

The funny part here is that when I'd first brought our little encounter up, I'd inadvertently started to bring up my perky lap-land friend. So by the time Megan had finished with her taut little speech, I was fully engaged with the First Hard-on of the Day. But in this case, three was definitely a crowd. I had no interest in Megan catching a glimpse of my unfortunate accident, so I put my arm across my leg, hoping she hadn't noticed just how unprofessional I can be.

"Sure, that's right. No problem there. No hard feelings." As soon as I said it, I had to suppress a laugh. No laughing at the hard feelings I was hiding with my arm. Megan had reestablished boundaries between us that probably never had been actually threatened by our unfortunate accident. A hard-on here was as out of place here as a trunk full of Hottentots. With hard-ons.

The thing is, it wasn't like I was all that attracted to Megan, because she was as contained and supervisor-like as ever. It's just that before our vodka-fest, the closest I'd been in a while to any sweet young thing was inadvertently bumping hips with some tight-skirted lassie on a crowded Muni. That one hadn't even bothered to glance at my foolishly friendly face. I was able to use that as fodder for a self-satisfaction session later, but sometimes those sessions aren't all that satisfying.

Mr. Happy settled down into his unsatisfied nest, and I kept driving. We hit the coast at Half Moon Bay, and I took a deep breath—it was a beautiful fall day, maybe 75, cloudless and clean. Even Megan seemed to loosen up a bit. We exchanged some bland pleasantries as we rolled by the collection of beautiful boutique state beaches, most of them requiring an entrance fee—but the views, those were free. When we came up on the little cove at Bean Hollow, I pulled over to pee.

Megan was out of the car when I came back from the Porta Potty, looking out from the small cliff to the waves. It was a nice scene, even in beige. From out of the blue, I had a burst of optimism. Maybe Megan and I can go back to being whatever we were before. Maybe Sun and I could go back to being whatever we were before—or at least for this visit. And maybe I'll just shoot myself, because when I turned the Studey over, it wouldn't start.

I turned it over again. Again. No. Megan hadn't gotten back in the car, but she had turned to look at me behind the wheel. I gave her a "no problem" wave, and tried again. Nada. What's scarier than your boss in a gossamer halter-top, five vodkas down? Your boss when she has a formal meeting to attend, and you are her driver.

She looked at her watch, and was at the driver's side window in a beige flash. "Hayden, there isn't a problem, is there? We need to be at the university in 45 minutes, and not a minute later."

"No problem, no problem. Just going to let it sit for a second; don't want to flood it." I looked out at her leaning in, those bird's-egg baby blues sharp on mine, her face a wall. "At worst, we could always hitchhike in."

She rose up from the window and crossed her arms over her chest. One word: "Hayden." Said in a monotone, my name with a good deal more gravity than it usually warranted. She stood unmoving, fixed on the impediment to a successful contract negotiation.

"OK, right, just a joke now." I turned it over and let it crank, battery be damned. The engine groaned, turning over more slowly, the starter's climb fading, but then it fluttered, caught, and clatteringly came to life, with a puff of gassy smoke. Megan came around and got in, and shut the door with a snap. She looked at her watch.

"Usually runs pretty good. But I've got these weaselly mechanics who are like out of a dime-store novel." I glanced at Megan, but she was back in her purse/lap/look-ahead five-dimensions away lockdown mode. Maybe not the best time to talk about my novel, but she was here, we were alone, and we had time.

"So, talking about novels, I'm not sure if you remember that I mentioned that I was writing one the other night. I know that I'm not that far into it, but it's moving along, but I don't know all that much about publishing." I glanced over at Megan. Lockdown continued.

"I know you were in publishing back in Boston, so maybe when I get a bit further along, maybe you could take a look at it?" When I said the word "look" it came out as a croak of sorts, but I left the sentence where it lay, bleeding.

Megan took an audible breath. She turned slightly toward me and said, "Hayden. Hayden, I worked for one of the most prestigious small presses in the country. Among our clients were Saul Bellow, John Gardner and Toni Morrison. We represented literary fiction, of psychological complexity and narrative development. I wouldn't know where to start with some kind of adventure tale." She lifted her purse and settled it quickly back in her lap. "Besides, that's my world no longer."

Stupid. Stupid on steroids. I'd vowed I wasn't going to bring up the novel again. Not until it was at least coming together as a story. It wasn't a novel now anyway. It was more a bunch of noises on paper. Stupid.

"Yeah. It is loosely based on *Brothers Karamazov* though. That's pretty literary. But it needs some polishing."

Tally time: I'd mentioned the novel to Megan twice now, both times without thinking. Two strikes. Time to take some pitches, or step out of the batter's box for a lifetime or two.

I took her right up to the administrative offices at UCSC without another word. There didn't seem to be many students around at all; classes were probably canceled because of the quake. When Megan was getting out of the car, I started to point out that she had a stain of some kind on her pants, but I caught myself. Small victories.

"I'll see you back here at 3," I said. Two hours to meet with Sun so that we could—what? I didn't have a clue, but just being back in Santa Cruz had given me a prickly feeling of anticipation and dread. Or maybe I was feeling happy—eagerly dreading my upcoming encounters with women was beginning to feel so normal, it was getting harder to tell what happy was.

THIRTEEN

....

I parked outside Sun's house and sat in the car. She lived— where *we* once lived—in a ramshackle two-bedroom beach bungalow on the Eastside, walking distance from the yacht harbor. Our house, yeah, *her* house, still had the chimney on, unlike a few other houses on the block. Probably would take more than a little shaker to bust coastal California real estate prices anyway. But she was just a renter, so what it was worth was meaningless. Even though I'm capable of thinking of meaningless stuff for hours on end, particularly when I'm scared of seeing, after a year's long absence, the woman I thought I'd spend my life with, sitting like a perv in my old car in front of her house probably wouldn't win any lost affection.

She answered the door barefoot, in torn Levis and a tight white t-shirt, makeupless, her thick hair loose. "Hay-den! You really did come." I was hanging back a bit, and the front porch was a fair piece lower than the step up into the house, but she reached out and kind of stroked my cheek, a bit of a soft slap or a cuff you might give to a dog you felt affection for. I leaned forward to give her a hug, but she had immediately turned and moved back to the living room, so I almost fell into the house. "C'mon in."

Nothing changed. Not much, anyway. A new/old overstuffed chair where the old/old one had been. Same ratty carpet. Same beautiful light from the high old windows. Same beautiful Sun. She sat on the old leather couch, the one we'd dragged over from a yard sale six houses down a couple of years ago. I sat down facing her on one of the hard chairs at the dining room table, though the dining room was just part of the big living room.

"So, what's happening? Did you get those CDs over to Will? I haven't seen him in months. You look good."

"Uh, thanks. No, haven't made it to Will's yet. House looks decent after the quake."

She flung a draping of hair over her shoulder and looked around. "Yep. Held steady. Like me. I've been holding steady." She looked at me, friendly but expressionless, a look I'd seen a thousand times, and one that always left me hungry.

"I'm really glad you weren't hurt. I was scared when I couldn't get in touch," I said.

I looked at her, looked around and looked back. This wasn't really moving in a direction I liked. But I didn't really have a direction in mind, so how could it move that way?

"Hey, no offense, but I was a little paranoid that your surfer guy was going to be here. Stupid, I know, but ..."

She smiled and got up. "Steve? What do you mean? He's here. He's just taking in some rays in the backyard. I can get him." She got up and walked into the small kitchen that looked out onto the backyard and I followed—but I *really* wish I hadn't.

Seems that Beach Boy Steve was having some kind of self-admiration society in the yard, and it was approaching a crescendo. He was sitting on the little lawn, shirt off and back to us, with his board shorts pulled down to about his knees. He had a big mirror in his lap. But that wasn't the main thing in his lap: he was working his rod hot and heavy with his right hand while he held the mirror with his left and admired his whack-off rhythm and his bad-boy abs.

That was way too much for me. I backed up and bumped into the refrigerator and then lurched back into the living room and sat down in the big chair. Sun made a weird squealing sound and shot out of the back door into the yard. I could hear them arguing for a couple of minutes, and I got up to leave. I was almost at the door when Sun spoke.

"Hayden, I want you to meet Steve, my boyfriend. Steve, this is Hay-den." Her face was flushed and she didn't smile, but she held it together. He stepped forward, tan, shirtless, golden-haired and buff, but thankfully wearing pants, and stretched out his hand.

"Hey dude, cool. Sun's told me good shit about you."

I looked at his hand for a mini-second, and then coughed loudly with my right hand at my face. I knew more about his hand than I wanted to. "Oh, sorry man," I said. "Bad cold; you don't want it. In fact, I should go so Sun doesn't get it either."

"OK dude. Catch you later."

I stepped out onto the front porch, and Sun came out and shut the door. "Hayden, I'm not even going to say anything about that. Steve's a good man, but that was way out of line. That will never happen again. Sorry."

She looked serious for a moment, and then she smiled her Sun smile, the one that always lit me up. I know it's corny to say, but it was a fact. I didn't really know how it ever got to this point. Maybe it was just a difference in philosophy, me being the philosophy major and all. We had both read *The Fountainhead* together at UC. I'd looked at it like it was a philosophical cartoon, but Sun swallowed it whole. She got into this whole Ayn Rand supremacy-of-the-individual blarney. Sun was always pretty even keel, but it drove her crazy one day when I said Rand's thoughts were Objectionably Objectivist. It became like a running joke between us.

She'd always had a kind of vague "let's all love one another" bent, but that left-leaning left town for a kind of weird lecture series at home, where I got vibed-up variations of *it's every woman for herself*, and *the less worthy are just going to be left behind*. But then she'd bring home a foster puppy, or give money to some skanky homeless dude downtown, but argue with me when I said that Ayn wouldn't approve. It was funny until it stopped being funny. We became kind of caricatures of ourselves in our arguments, at last reaching the point where we were people in a long-running play, tired of our lines. That's when I left.

So, the day was moving along well: I'd blown it again with Megan about setting up a discussion of my novel, and my big interaction with Sun was running from her boyfriend's whack-happy handshake. This day was shaping up to be a real barnburner. What would my afternoon gift be?

FOURTEEN

::

Megan sat on a bench to the side of the university's administrative offices, shaded by a leafy oak. She sat as she had in Hayden's car, upright, purse in her lap, held with both hands. The small parking lot had few cars and little movement; Megan barely moved as well. When a young woman dressed in a tight yellow dress walked in front of her on her way into the building, Megan stirred.

She glanced around, opened her purse, and quickly snapped it shut. Though there was no sun in her eyes, she appeared to be squinting, her lips drawn up toward her pinched eyes. She glanced around again, opened the purse, and pulled out a plastic airline-size bottle of vodka. She wrapped that in a paisley silk handkerchief and brought it to her face and drank. To a passerby, it might have appeared that she was vigorously scrubbing her face, the handkerchief bobbing up and down with the movements from her hand and mouth.

Finished, she daubed at the corners of her lips with the handkerchief, wrapped up the bottle, and put both back into her purse. She slowly moved her head across the range of her vision, scanning the parking lot, and then shifted to turn and look up at the office building. She settled back on the bench, purse in lap, expression-less. Hayden showed up five minutes later.

"So boss, how'd it go? Did you get them to extend the lease until 2020? Is it bonus time?"

Megan eased into the car, glanced at Hayden and then put on her seat belt. "It's hard to say if it went anywhere, Hayden. The board of directors debated the issue with me both in the meeting and outside of it, and then they tabled the discussion until the next quarter. Right now the contract is in suspension." She rubbed the back of her neck and turned to Hayden. "Is there somewhere here we can get a meal? They had these wretched little finger sand-wiches in there, something fishy, and the odor alone made me sit on the other side of the table. I'm quite hungry."

"Huh, sorry about the contract. But yeah, we can go to one of my old hangouts, College Eight Café. It's not Paris, but they have sandwiches, and some don't swim."

Megan rubbed her neck again. *Always with the jokes,* she thought. *I suppose it's better than being around a consistently gloomy person. But maybe not that much better.*

They had been in the crowded café for fifteen minutes, Megan picking at a roast beef sandwich that seemed to have been dried on a clothesline, and Hayden wolfing a bowl of minestrone soup, when some yelling broke out behind them. A very tall young black woman was standing at a table, leaning toward an older seated black man, whose back was to Megan's table. She had a small, brightly colored cloth handbag in her hand, with which she punched at the air when she spoke.

"I don't care, I don't care!" shouted the young woman. "Why did you even come here at all? I haven't had a father for years!" She leaned forward toward the man, putting both hands on the table surface. She said in a much calmer voice, but one that could still be overheard in the now-quiet café, "You might be somebody's father, but not mine!" She stood up and whirled around, almost stumbled, and walked quickly out of the café.

Megan was sitting catty-corner to their table, while Hayden had had to turn almost completely around to look at the commotion. Hayden turned back to his table and Megan started to move her glance back to him when the older man put his head in his hand while he sat, turning his head more in profile to Megan. She gasped.

"It's Mr. Reed!" she said, leaning in to Hayden. "It's the homeless man that stands outside our building, the one with the artificial leg. I had a conversation with him the other day; he'd been beaten up." She stared at Jacob, looked back at Hayden, and looked back to Jacob.

Hayden turned around again and focused on Jacob, peering intently. "Oh yeah, it's him. I can see the edge of that leg where his pants are pulled up. It's Leg Man, all right. Wow, he's even wearing a tie."

Megan winced and leaned in to Hayden. "Leg Man!" she whispered, her lips drawn back. "That's what you call him? His name is Mr. Jacob Reed. He was reading Bronte before some hooligans tore up the novel. Hayden, why is he even here? And who is that woman?"

Hayden expelled a breath through pursed lips. "Well, beats me. Maybe with Consolidated closed he hitchhiked down here to check out the begging scene. Maybe he was trying to get that girl to buy him lunch. Who knows?" Hayden crumpled up his napkin and put it in the center of his empty bowl. "Anyway, we should head back up to the City. I have a few things I need to do."

Megan looked quickly in her purse and pulled out her wallet, putting some bills on top of the check. She looked in the wallet again, paused and then put it back in her purse. "I don't believe that giving the homeless money actually does them any good," she said in a low tone. "But I spoke to Mr. Reed just two days ago, and he seemed to be a reasonable man. I don't want to impose on you Hayden, but I believe we should offer him transportation back to San Francisco."

Hayden had started to get up to leave, but then he sat back down, glanced over his shoulder at Jacob and shook his head. "Well, Jesus, I mean, sorry, but we don't even know that guy. We don't even know if he needs a ride. What if he was just hassling that girl because hassling people is his thing? What if he's nuts?"

"He is not 'nuts,' as you put it. He was reading *Wuthering Heights*. We had a conversation about Bronte." She raised her head at Hayden, pushing her chin forward.

Hayden raised both hands a little off the table, and then brought them together in a soft slap. "OK. OK, Megan. If you want to check him out and see if he needs a ride, that's fine. You're the boss. But he's sitting behind you on the way back."

She stood up and started to walk over to Jacob. When she rose, she set her purse closer to Hayden. She hadn't snapped the clasp properly, and it opened a little. Hayden looked down and saw the neck of the miniature vodka bottle pushed up out of the handkerchief. He looked up at Megan, who was moving around the table in front of Jacob, and he pushed the handkerchief a little to the side. Another little vodka bottle came into sight.

Megan arrived at Jacob's table, her face flushed. She stuck out her hand. "Mr. Reed, I believe you'll remember me. Megan Thornstock from Consolidated. We had a conversation in the passageway behind the building the other day."

Jacob rose slowly, hands on hips. He sighed and said, "Yes, I remember." He extended his hand and gave Megan a quick, soft handshake. "I'm sorry, I've just had a discussion with my daughter that's gotten out of hand, and it shook me up."

Megan backed slightly and put her hand on top of a chair. "I'm sorry to disturb you when family matters are pressing, but I wanted to ensure that you had transportation back to San Francisco." Inclining her head toward Hayden, she said, "I'm not sure if you've met Hayden MacNamara, Consolidated's copyeditor, but he and I are about to return to San Francisco after our meetings today, and we're happy to offer you a ride."

Jacob looked over at Hayden, who raised his hand and smiled. Jacob smoothed his old tie down his chest and nodded, then picked up a worn backpack. "You can call me Jacob, Megan. I appreciate the offer, and I will accept it. Man takes the right ride, no matter the timing." He said this without smiling, and then before Megan and Hayden were ready, he walked out the door.

FIFTEEN

···

*S*hitty day. Damn shitty day, Jacob thought. *I might as well be dead as far as Tabby's concerned. Wouldn't even tell me about her brother. Well, maybe Josh doesn't hate me as much.* He looked over his shoulder at Megan and Hayden catching up to him as he walked on the path outside the café. *These people. Almost like I'm haunted, them here. What's the devil got up his sleeve, putting us all in that restaurant?*

"There's a parking lot just down the hill, sir. I mean Mr. Reed. My car's in the lot," said Hayden, who waved his hand toward nothing.

"Not a sir. Mr. Reed's OK if that works for you, but the name's Jacob."

They were walking down a narrow path that flanked a road, the clustered campus trees cutting the sun for most of the way. Hayden didn't answer for a minute, started to speak and stopped, and then when he did answer, his words didn't seem to hook properly to the preceding words.

"OK. I'm Hayden. I mean, Megan said that I'm Hayden, but I'm Hayden. OK."

Jacob looked back over his shoulder at Hayden and nodded. Kid's nervous. Blonde's obviously his boss. Maybe something else too.

When Hayden pointed to his car in the parking lot, Jacob said, "A Studebaker? My oh my, yes. A Studebaker." He laughed.

Hayden started to tell him about his history with the car, but Jacob only nodded, saying nothing, and Hayden quieted down. Hayden headed toward town, and then took the freeway ramp onto Highway 17. No one spoke for more than 30 minutes, until Megan turned to Jacob in the back seat.

"Did you ever finish Wuthering Heights? If I recall, you were deep into the novel, where a lot of the emotional subtext is surfacing."

Jacob shifted in the back seat, and took a deep breath. He appeared not to have heard Megan, but then he leaned forward slightly and said, "Sorry, off in a daydream. The book. Yes, you'd told me about all the sisters, the writers. No. No, didn't finish; it was too torn up after that situation with those punks. Shame."

Megan quickly turned fully around to face Jacob. "It is a shame! And I hope the police catch up with those criminals. But don't you want to know how the work concludes?"

"The book? Well, sure. Maybe I could just go to the library and pick it up. I do check out books now and then." Jacob scratched his head and looked out at a large mall that they were passing. This one's got the book bee in her bonnet. *Better than thinking about lost children, I suppose.*

"Yes, the library is a good resource, yes," said Megan. "But let me look into it. Perhaps I have an extra copy. I'd be happy to give you some of my impressions of the work as well."

Jacob grunted from the back, a sound that could be interpreted as "yes," if the hearer were inclined in that direction. The car fell back into the drone of an old car's engine, until Hayden turned on the radio, and began moving rapidly up and down the dial. He paused on a song for a moment, and then moved on. When he heard Jackie Wilson's "Lonely Teardrops" he left it on, and turned it up loud.

He looked slightly over his shoulder, paused, and then said, "This is a good one."

Jacob said, "Yeah. Jackie Wilson. You don't mind turning it down, though?"

"Oh, no, sure," said Hayden, who turned it down so it could barely be heard. "I thought you might like some R&B stuff, you know, some good R&B."

Jacob sighed. "Well, R&B, yeah. I'm tired though. If you find any stations with Lester Young or Dexter Gordon, you turn that right back up." Jacob put his backpack at an angle between the top of the seat and the window, and leaned back against it, closing his eyes. *R&B. Kid means well, I guess. Maybe I should have told him to find the*

Mozart station, just to blow his mind about the scruffy black guy in his backseat.

Jacob listened to the tinny scratching from the radio that folded in with the old engine's drone. Eyes shut, he remembered how not long after the war, before he let the drink define him, tiny Tabitha would bring him old vinyl records from the shelf and ask him to play them. She liked jazz too, but since all of Jacob's records were jazz, she didn't have much choice. *Tabby looked good, real good. Tall. Didn't find much good to say to her old man though. Might have been a lot better to try a phone call first.* He grimaced and settled back against his makeshift pillow, but he knew nothing could make him sleep.

They came into San Francisco as the sun was softening in the sky. Hayden was heading up 280 toward downtown when Jacob spoke up from the back. "If it's no trouble, could you drop me off somewhere near Market and Powell?"

"Yeah, I think—" said Hayden.

Megan turned around to the back seat. "Well, have you relocated from that, um, place behind the Consolidated building, Mr. Reed? I'm sure the fall nights are beginning to get a little drafty, so I hope you're in a more suitable dwelling," she said.

Jacob laughed an easy, free laugh that lightly trailed off. "Oh, I'm in a suitable dwelling, all right. Suits me fine. I've worked with wind for years; I know its ways. Don't trouble yourself about me."

"Oh. Well, I hope that means everything is better. And I hope you resolve whatever was the point of contention between you and the young woman in the restaurant," Megan said.

There was silence in the car. Jacob looked out the window at a crowded Muni, stopped to take on more riders. He scratched his face and scowled. "As I said, the young woman was my daughter. Family issue. That's going to take several buckets of resolving."

"Yes. I don't mean to pry. I do hope everything works out."

Just then, Hayden pulled into an empty bus stop across from the Flood Building. Jacob peered out the window, seeing Sully leaning back against the building, the white beard appearing to glow in the waning sun.

"Everything is too many things to work out; I'll start with one thing. I do appreciate the ride."

He stepped out of the car but leaned back in before he closed the door, and said to Megan, "I hope things work out for you too. Goodbye." He moved to the traffic signal, into a small crowd, mostly tourists and business people getting off work.

Jacob didn't look back at their car when it passed through the light and on up Market.

SIXTEEN

....

We dropped Leg Man off by the old Woolworth's building, and I headed back up Market, moving toward Megan's place.

"Well, what do you think he meant by that?" Megan said.

I didn't answer. I didn't have a real clue about what things for Megan needed working out, and I'd already said too much. But that didn't stop me from saying just a bit more a minute later.

"Wow," I said. "I wonder what Leg Man's story is? And what he did to his daughter to make her scream like that?"

Megan audibly sniffed. "Hayden, *Leg Man,* really! His name, again, is Jacob Reed. I hope I don't have to mention it again. He is a homeless man, but he is intelligent." She turned in the seat toward me and shades of my fourth-grade teacher, actually waggled her finger at me as she spoke. "It's difficult to ascertain what the circumstances are with his daughter, but family issues are complex." She settled back into her seat and I could hear her quick intake of breath. "Matters between fathers and daughters are very complex."

I cut up Powell and headed up toward Taylor. No way I was getting out of the car and going into that apartment this time though. *I'd* probably end up wearing the parachute-pants outfit if I did. So I avoided that humiliation. However, you can't avoid them all, and I didn't. When I dropped Megan off outside the Belvedere, right when she was getting out of the car, I said, "Strange day, but you're safe now. And I see they've cleaned up most of the earthquake debris from around the place. Probably could relax with a couple more shots of vodka without the place falling down on you."

I was leaning across the seat when I said that, and Megan poked her head back in so quickly that I had to back up. She tilted her head to the side and squinted. "Hayden, what exactly do you mean by that?"

"Well, I didn't mean anything. I just meant that you could relax. I know it's been a lousy day for you, with the contract and all. I saw you'd eased it on down a bit with a little eye-opener, when you'd left your purse on the table at the café. I get it, big-time, no problem."

She climbed back into the car and sat on the edge of the seat, with her feet out on the curb and her head turned back to me. "You looked in my purse? You went through my purse, Hayden? And what precisely do you 'get'?"

I yanked on the skin around my Adam's apple; weird habit I have when I get nervous. "No, I didn't go through your purse, it just fell open and I looked in. Not snooping. I don't get anything." I looked away from her and up the street, and put my hands on the wheel so I could grip something. "I mean, it's easy to see how a drink can relax you when you're tense. I mean relax everybody, all of us."

Megan hadn't taken her eyes off me. "Hayden, it's not clear what you're getting at, but what is clear is that you seem to be losing the understanding of our boundaries. We've already gone through the incident at my apartment, and I truly refuse to speak of that again. Today's contract negotiations were arduous, and I happened to have that bottle in my purse from a flight I took some weeks back."

She pulled at a clump of hair and then pushed it over her shoulder, and scowled. She got out of the car and leaned her head back in. "I contacted Consolidated from the university. We return to work tomorrow. I have one-hundred percent expectation that you and I will resume our normal business lives, and we won't have to discuss your peculiar interpretations of events again. I very much appreciate your driving today."

She shut the door with a crisp stroke. Not a slam, but a sharp Meganistic snap.

So, that went well. Between Sun and Megan, in one day I'd alienated around half of the women I know. But the day's not over yet—maybe I should give Diana a call and see if I can go three-for-three? Or maybe I should just go home.

I headed for the Haight. There were still many, many piles of earthquake leavings on the streets. At California and Divisadero, there was the biggest dumpster I'd ever seen, like a dumpster ocean liner, filled with what looked like busted-up building materials. The weird thing is that there was a dressmaker's dummy riding on the very top of some lumber and someone had put a straw hat on it, with what looked like real yellow flowers. San Francisco.

Megan's got something going with the booze. I could hear that clink of ice on the phone the other night. And I like a good pop myself, but that's weird about the little bottles in her purse. I mean, it wouldn't be all that weird if one of my friends were doing it, but Megan? That's a spreadsheet wearing a miniskirt. Must be a lot of work pressure, but she's pretty touchy about it. But I think I've set back my hope to get her to look at my novel about a thousand years.

Before I was even halfway up the stairs, I could hear Drew coughing in the kitchen. His cough had become this resonant thing, deep in his chest, and he panted a bit when he really got going. He was really going now. I went into the kitchen and he was bent over the sink, clutching a glass of water. He wasn't throwing up, but his whole body shook when he coughed.

"Hey man, that cough hasn't gotten any better at all. Are you OK? I think it's time you saw somebody about it—you might have pneumonia or something like that."

I moved alongside the sink and leaned against the L-shape of the countertop, and looked at Drew, who hadn't come up yet from the sink. He went through another series of wracking breaths, and then turned to me, his face a blazing red, as were his eyes. He had a couple of big, raised bruises too, one near his temple and one at his hairline.

"I know. Pretty bad, huh?" He choked out the words, and took a long drink of water. Drew was never a robust guy, but he was looking drawn. "You're right about the doc, though. I'll go to the clinic tomorrow."

"Good. But did you take a shot from someone with a pool cue at the bar? Your head looks like you used it to open a safe."

He scratched his close-cropped hair near the hairline bruise and laughed, which thankfully didn't get him coughing again. "Actually, I think I did that when I was moving a bunch of flowers out to the alley behind the bar and the door hit me on the side of the head. I didn't think it hit me that hard, but I woke up with the bruises this morning. With that and the cough, I'm quite a catch."

"You keep coughing like that and you'll need someone to catch you. Anyway, I'm going to put my feet up for a little while before dinner. It's been a weird day."

I headed back toward my room, but turned back to the kitchen and said, "You seen Roland? Has he made a peep lately?" Roland's door, as always, remained the shut, silent sentinel defending his lair.

Drew smiled and said, "I did. We sort of even ate lunch together, because he ate lunch in his room with the door open. I asked him how it was going and he said 'fine.' He was working on that weird filming system he has. He *can* still speak."

"Good to know," I said. "I'll test him next time I see him." I moved into my room to try and not think of my day's triumphs.

SEVENTEEN

Megan had turned several pages of *Middlemarch* before she realized that nothing of the reading had stuck in her head. It was one of three first editions she owned, her only Eliot first, a heavy book with a tooled leather cover of forest green, with gold lettering. Eliot's acknowledged best, but Megan always felt more companionship from *Adam Bede,* the first Eliot work she'd read, years ago. But *Middlemarch* was one of the volumes she turned to for comfort, its heft a reassuring ballast.

She brought the book up to her chest and exhaled slowly. She looked around the living room, the fading light giving the ornamental frieze a cold look. Propped up on her couch, big pillows behind her, she noticed that one of her feet was on her purse. *Hayden and the bottles. I hope we won't deal with that tedium again.*

She grabbed the purse and took out both the empty bottle and the full one. She started to unscrew the cap on the full bottle, but then sighed and went into the kitchen. *I should make a proper drink out of this and not fall into an unfortunate pattern.* She made herself a small vodka tonic and returned to the couch.

She had taken several sips of her third drink when she thought of Jacob. *He seems so forlorn. Perhaps he is losing his daughter, or has lost her.* She got up and went to the biggest bookshelf, but not finding what she sought, moved to the heavy cabinet with the glass doors, a miracle survivor of the quake. There it was. The nice clothbound copy of *Wuthering Heights.* Not one of her rarities, nothing that she couldn't spare. *Mr. Reed could probably use a Bronte for company.* She got up and went to the door, book in hand.

She walked the few blocks up to Consolidated from the Muni stop. The day had cooled considerably, and with night rounding the corner, small droplets of fog dampened her long coat. It was well past five, and the area's business traffic was thinning. She rocked a little bit on the medium heels she was wearing and slowed when she approached the alley. *What will I do if he's in that little cave? I don't think I should knock on that. Maybe I can just drop the book off near that pile of his belongings. Perhaps this isn't the best idea.*

She rounded the corner of the alley and saw Jacob standing near his makeshift tent, fussing with the zipper of a faded U.S. Army jacket that he held. He looked up when he heard the click of Megan's heels and raised his eyebrows. He set the jacket on the housing for the electrical box and turned to face her.

"Mr. Reed, I'm glad to see you are here. I have something for you." She spoke much more loudly than was necessary, even though she was still twenty feet away. She raised the large book over her head, feeling breathless. He moved forward a step and cocked his head.

"Megan, there's no reason to be coming out here, on the edge of night. This area can get funny after night falls. What's that?"

"Oh, it's the book, the Bronte book!" Megan giggled, a high trilling sound that caused her to cover her mouth with her other hand. "I mean, it's *Wuthering Heights,* the book we were discussing. I brought you one of my copies so you could finish it."

She pushed the book out at arm's length toward Jacob, her hand trembling a little at the wrist. Jacob peered into her face for a moment before he took the book. "Well. Can't say as I actually thought you'd bring me this. I wouldn't mind working through it, though I think there's only pain to come for that couple."

Megan smiled, the thick glasses jumping a little on her brow. She spoke rapidly, nodding her head with each sentence. "Yes, trouble there will be, plenty of trouble! Not just for Heathcliff and Catherine, though, but Catherine's Catherine, and Isabella and all of the—oh, I don't know how far along you are. But the troubles are Bronte's means of pulling away the curtains of human character. But even with the curtains drawn, it's dark."

Jacob looked at her and leaned against the electrical cabinet. He pursed his lips. "Megan, I appreciate the book. I will return it to you after I'm finished. But I'm going to ask you something: how much drinking are you doing? Are you just having a drink or two at home after work, or is that just a warm-up?" He crossed his hands over the book, which was tucked into his stomach while he leaned back against the cabinet.

Megan stiffened and pulled at a hank of hair at her collar. She leaned forward to speak, stopped and then rose up slightly on her heels. "Mr. Reed, that's no question—I mean *really!* How is it your concern, I mean, there's no drinking issue! I don't have a drinking issue." Megan was breathing rapidly and she felt her eyes tearing up. *Why would he ask me that?* She swiped quickly at one corner of her eye and looked around for a place to sit, but there wasn't one.

"Whoa girl, no need to get worked up! I'm not trying to butt into your business. I'm just a guy that's had his own liquor situation. Nobody said you were in trouble."

Megan held her lower lip under her upper, because it had began to tremble. "There's no trouble—" she said, her voice barely audible.

Jacob began flipping randomly through the pages of *Wuthering Heights,* stopping to scan some words on some pages, only to flip rapidly ahead or behind. He didn't raise his head when he spoke again. "I had a problem. A big problem. Cut some blood out of me to stop the problem. Nobody could tell me nothing about it, either. It was *my* problem. So I'm not saying anything about your situation. All I'm saying is that I've had a lot of time to think about my own business. If you ever want to discuss anything, my office is open." He looked up and smiled.

"Mr. Reed, honestly, I mean I shouldn't even be talking about my personal life, but honestly, I have a lot of pressure in my work, and I occasionally have a drink or two at home to relax. There's nothing elaborate or sinister about it. I can handle the pressure."

She looked up the alley to Market, where a man in a dark suit walked quickly by. It was nearly dark; the street was illumined with car lights and streetlamps. "I really should go. Please take your time with the book. I'll be back at work as of tomorrow and ever after that, should you want to return it. Goodbye."

She nodded at Jacob and moved quickly off, though her gait was still unsteady. *Why would he bring up drinking? I was perfectly coherent this evening. Could Hayden have said something about that vodka bottle? But Hayden and Mr. Reed weren't even alone after that. Of course, I have read that alcoholism is rampant among the homeless. Perhaps it's an issue they always bring up.*

She walked to the Muni stop and stood, holding her purse to her chest. Tiny droplets in the fog lit on her blond hair, which sparkled under a streetlight.

EIGHTEEN

....

Consolidated. Cubes all in a row, bad art back on the walls, fluorescents still flourishing. No broken glass, no glugging Sparkletts bottles on the rug, no zombies passing as employees. And the prez had got McManus, our Vice President of Portly, to stand at the double doors and greet everyone with a hearty, "Very good to see you! It's good to be back up and running, isn't it?"

Since McManus's speaking voice was like a tuba with dynamite, he scared most everyone who entered the door, and most of them looked pretty scared anyway. People didn't go immediately to their cubes; they were milling about in little hives, which broke up, and then reassembled again with slightly different constituents.

I didn't feel like greeting anyone. I wondered if I was the only one that felt like maybe it would have been better if old Consolidated took a bigger hit from the quake, maybe requiring some structural repairs that might take two weeks, a month. Somehow, proofing complex and ruthlessly over-worded leasing documents just didn't have the sparkle it once had. I sat in my cleaned cube like a bright block of tofu and thought that it was a sure thing that Faulkner had never proofread a leasing contract.

One solid, though: After I booted my computer, the first thing I checked was my novel. It was alive, even if the plot was lying on its side. That's a plus.

And I did have the distraction of a new milling hive within eyesight of my cube: Silvie, Crenshaw and Diana clustered near the aisle that led down to the lawyers' offices. I was gratified to see that Diana didn't think that the first day back on the job after a disaster merited any modesty: she wore a black skirt that looked like a weird cross between suede and vinyl; it might have had enough fabric for two decent-sized hankies. On top she had a tight red sweater that was mohair or dragon's hair or something, because it was all wispy and fluttery. I thought I should go and rally the troops.

"So, nobody looks the worse for wear, considering a building essentially fell on us," I said.

Diana smiled and said, "Hey Hayden." Sylvie spun toward me and grimaced. "That's not all that funny Hayden. There could still be aftershocks. It's only been a week, you know." Crenshaw just rocked on his heels and grinned. He was a good grinner.

"Hey Syl, that's no way to talk to the boss. I could easily arrange so that all of Rexroth's contracts went to you, if you're not careful."

Rexroth was the office lawyer who was truly a pain in the ass, and considering the stiff competition, he had some real ass-paining skills. His contracts were the most abstruse bogs of impenetrable prose, and naturally, he took the most umbrage when we tried to make them comprehensible.

Sylvie raised her head and flicked a bangled wrist at me, a queen dismissing a pageboy. I was her boss, but I kept things pretty casual, which is how I wanted it. Both Sylvie and Crenshaw were solid employees, and allies besides. Diana was another matter. Diana I wanted like a boy wants birthday cake. Diana made me stupid.

"So, Diana, don't you live just off the Marina? Did your house do OK?"

She turned fully to me and said, "One cracked window, that's it. Yeah, I live off of Laguna, near Chestnut. Some houses were pretty trashed." She flicked her head to shift her hair off her shoulder and said, "You can still smell the burnt places, no matter where you walk."

I'd been mostly looking at her eyes while she was talking and glancing at those luscious lips. I knew better to even let my eyes flit to the lovely gifts that that sweater was concealing. I was very conscious of her scent, something a little sweet, a little musky. But when she flicked her head, it reminded me so much of Megan's similar gesture on quake-night at her apartment that it set me back a step.

"Yeah, wow, I know. It was hard-core down there, for sure," I said.

Sylvie started looking over her shoulder and I knew that she was about to leave, and that when she did, Crenshaw would follow. He was a bit like a little brother for her, and happily let her boss him around, though they were peers.

"I'm going to return to the fascinating Edbrook project. With all this time away, it's like a brand new nightmare," said Sylvie. She shook a bangly, jangly arm and headed toward her cube. Crenshaw followed without a word. Diana and I both mumbled something at them.

Well, it's now or never.

"Hey Diana, I was thinking that you and I—"

"Hayden, could I see you in my office? Sorry Diana, but it can't wait." Megan's voice from behind startled me enough to make my casual-dude-leaning-against-office-wall approach snap back to an almost military posture. She swept by us without looking, a motion machine in thin pinstripes.

"Uh, yeah, be right there. Sorry Diana, but I'll catch you later."

Diana looked in Megan's direction and whispered, "I think you're in trouble. Bye."

Crap. How long will it be before I can muster it up to ask her out now? And trouble? With Megan? Surely you jest. We're old buddies now. I sighed and walked down to my old buddy's office. Expecting trouble.

I entered Megan's office, which had returned to its standard sense of ordered perfection: dust bunnies, abandon hope, all ye who enter here. Megan looked up from a large stack of papers and said, "Hayden. Please shut the door and sit down."

I closed, I sat, I worried. "Hayden, I recognize that things have been irregular between us since the earthquake. I know we have resolved those issues through our conversations. However, the unusual circumstances have set in motion a couple of things that are outside the work purview." She held up the silver-cased pen that she'd been writing with, and fixed her gaze on it.

"So. I have a request that is more personal than professional. And of course, you are free to refuse it, no harm done."

I think my swallowing must have sounded like a bad pipe; at least it did to me. "Well, sure. I mean, what do you have in mind?"

"I've taken a small interest in Mr. Reed's welfare. Now you saw that there has been some disagreement between he and his daughter. I'd like you to deliver a message to his daughter through your Santa Cruz contact. Can you do that for me?" She looked up expectantly and gave me a small smile.

"OK, his daughter. You mean have Sun—Sun, that's my friend's name—have Sun go up to the college and find that girl and tell her something? I'm not sure I understand. Sun doesn't even know her. And she doesn't know where to find her. I mean, we don't even know Leg Man's daughter's name."

Megan's nostrils flared. "Hayden! I truly wish *not* to ask of you again. The man's name is Jacob Reed. Please don't call him 'Leg Man' again. Ever." She took a breath and pulled a folder across her desk "Now, I will find out the woman's name and where to deliver the message. It's necessary that it is a handwritten message, from me, and I want it delivered to her by another young woman, as you've described your friend. This is a personal matter, and I don't want it to be a matter of the United States mail."

She smiled a quick smile. "Well, do you think that's possible?"

"Sure, I guess it's possible. It's just a little weird. Not exactly weird, but you don't really know any of these people. But yeah, I'll check with Sun and get back to you."

I stood up and turned a little too quickly, so that I sharply kneed the hard edge of the swivel chair I'd been sitting on. "Shit," I said, teeth clenched. Every time I tried to be direct and assertive, to try and match Megan, I got some message from the universe that said *no*.

Megan spoke as I opened the door. "Hayden, thank you. I hope you don't feel I'm imposing on you. But it's for a good reason."

I nodded and left. Before the quake, I would have been assured that Megan's reasons were always good reasons. I'd wondered before if she'd ever made a mistake. But now, I wasn't too sure of Megan or her motives. At all. However, this gave me an excuse to talk to Sun. That's me, always looking on the bright side. Surely I had the skills to really tangle up all of us in this mess, whatever it was.

I went back to my cube and sat. I had four contracts that hadn't been touched, one that had been sitting on my desk when the world went topsy-turvy on quake day. I'd been told by one of the junior legal beagles that there were at least three more in the pipeline, hip-hip-hooray. By the end of the day, I'd gone through the one in earthquake stasis, two more from the inbox, and assigned another two to Sylvie and Crenshaw. I couldn't tell you one word about the content of those contracts. Mostly I'd been moving my red pen over lines on paper, and thinking about Sun, Megan and Diana. And Leg Man. Oh, I mean Mr. Reed.

You'd be surprised—or maybe not—how passionately I wished there was some beer at home.

NINETEEN

··

Four mornings later, a cool, cloudy Friday in the City. Jacob was panhandling outside the big technical bookstore a few doors down from Consolidated. He occasionally went inside to look at the big architectural design and engineering books, which had interested him since high school. *Building's got a soul, just like a person,* he used to say to the members of his squad, back in wartime. One time, T-Bone, a crazy white kid from Illinois, told him that the only buildings that had souls were haunted. He just laughed. No one laughed the next day when T-Bone got lit up in a firefight on the edge of a rice paddy, where three other guys got torn up pretty bad. T-Bone didn't have a chance to know how torn up he'd gotten.

But the bookstore owner, kind of a crazy white guy himself, but old, didn't mind that Jacob panhandled outside. He'd even stepped out before and had a conversation about the old Flood Building down on Market, and about flying buttresses and columns and cornices. He'd seen Jacob in the architecture books a few times, and liked the subject himself.

Jacob had been working the street for less than an hour when he heard someone speak from the side. "Mr. Reed, do you have a moment?"

Uhh, that Megan woman again. What now? He turned to Megan just as she was moving past his leg on the sidewalk, to which she gave a wide berth. "Mr. Reed, I hope you don't mind, but it will only be a minute."

She was wearing a pinkish kind of pantsuit thing, with what looked like tiny black pebbles all over the suit, and she carried a black briefcase. *Loaded for bear. In pink.*

"Yes Megan, hello. I'm not quite finished with the book yet, but—"

"No, no, it's not about your book, it's about your daughter." She set the briefcase on the sidewalk and smiled.

Jacob's heart rolled. "My daughter? What's wrong? Is something wrong with Tabby?"

"No, nothing's wrong, nothing at all. It's just that, well, I sent her a message, and I think you might be hearing from her soon." She swallowed hard and glanced at Jacob, and then glanced away.

Jacob hop-stepped over to his leg and quickly strapped it on. He moved back in front of Megan and said, "I don't understand you. What kind of message? And why would you even send a message? You don't know my daughter." He moved close to Megan, looking into her eyes, his thick eyebrows pushed down by his furrowed brow.

"Yes. I mean no, I don't really know her. What I mean is that I understood that there were some difficulties between you and your daughter. And I understand when fathers and daughters are out of sorts. I mean, my father is a good man, a very good man, but—well, I needn't go on about my father ..." She smoothed her hair on both sides of her face and tugged her blouse down.

Jacob stared. He involuntarily drew a sharp intake of breath, and then released it audibly out of his nose. He held his hands up at waist height. "I don't know where to begin," he said. He expelled a long breath. "Megan, I'm not even sure how we got to where we're at here. You're in your building, in your pink suit, and I'm in the alley with my old coat. And my daughter is at the university with her friends. Now I'm not sure why a woman who doesn't even know me would be coming round anyway, much less putting herself into any business with my daughter."

Megan took a white handkerchief from her purse and cleaned her glasses with it, though they didn't need cleaning. She finished and said, "Mr. Reed—Jacob—it must seem rather inconceivable, and that I'm meddling where I shouldn't be. That might be true. It's just that, well, I thought your daughter looked like a fine person, and that you seem to be a fine person too." She took the handkerchief out again, and began polishing, looking away from Jacob. "It seemed to me that there must be a solution, and I took it upon myself."

Jacob tightly held the sides of his coat away from his body. "A solution! You don't even know what the problem is! You don't know Tabitha and you don't know me! You don't know anything! You don't even recognize your own problem, much less have a solution!"

Megan backed up a step and half of another, rocking a little on the pink heels. She nodded and started to speak, but then turned and started walking up Market toward Consolidated. She walked about five steps and then turned back to Jacob. "I hope you are enjoying the Bronte, Mr. Reed. And you might hear from your daughter anyway. I apologize for the interference."

Jacob said nothing. Megan continued toward Consolidated and Jacob watched as she entered the building. *What is with that woman? Fifteen minutes in a café with Tabby and she wants to set us right? Some other business with her father part of it?* Jacob walked over to the side of the bookstore building, where the stone supports afforded a small ledge. He leaned against it for a while, not seeing the milling business traffic, nor smelling the pungent aroma of fresh coffee from a street cart. *Might have to give Tabby a call again.*

He unstrapped his leg and moved it into the sidewalk and then returned back to the bookstore front. Almost immediately, an older woman walking a tiny dog threw a handful of change into the leg's pocket. She nodded grimly at Jacob and walked on. *That one proba-bly lives around here. Not a tourist.* He clenched his jaw and then rubbed it with a calloused palm. *But who am I kidding? I don't under-stand people, just like they don't understand me.*

TWENTY

"Sun, hey, I know it's early, but do you have a minute?"

"Hay-den, that's funny, I was going to call you! The note, right? I did deliver it; you won't believe what's happened since."

Oh, I probably would. Maybe Sun and Tabitha had robbed a bank together, or they'd started a bakery that was going to be profiled on 60 *Minutes* next week, or something. Sun had a way of falling into things. And she was usually the one that stayed on her feet after the fall.

"Oh, OK, so you did talk to her? Does she have any message for her father?"

"Yeah, that her father is an asshole!" She laughed loudly, in that weird rising trill of hers that would have been completely obnoxious, were it not so natural. And were she not pop-your-eyeballs beautiful.

"Yeah, but that's not the thing. The thing is that she and I have been hanging out. A lot. We met at Saturn the first time and ended up staying for a few hours. We've been like hanging out every couple of days since then. She's really into yoga, and started coming into the studio. We might even do an art thing together for one of her assignments. She's great."

"Oh, well, good. But she doesn't have a message for her dad? It's weird, but like I said, my boss set this up and I'm supposed to get any message back to her dad, through my boss."

Sun sighed into the phone. "I told you: the message is that he's an *asshole.* I'm not kidding. And from how she's told me, he *is* an asshole. Or at least a dead drunk who pretty much left his family for a barstool. She doesn't want anything to do with him."

This wasn't going exactly where I wanted it to. I mean, it was lousy that Leg Man's daughter had crapped out on him, or maybe he had done the first round of crapping, but I was hoping that would be some positive news so that I might look good with Megan, and maybe even bring her back around to talking about literature. My literature. And sure, I was also thinking that maybe this might be an opening for Sun and I to re-connect somewhere. Why not shoot the moon?

"Yeah," I said. "He seems pretty OK though. I don't think he's a drunk. I mean, I don't hang out with him or anything, but I see him all the time, and he never seems drunk. He is a homeless guy though."

"Right. He can't even get off the streets. And he wants his beautiful, smart daughter to hang with him? What are they going to do, go dumpster-diving together?" She laughed again, the song of it rolling off.

"That's pretty harsh, Sun. He is her father. I don't even know the guy, but he's not an asshole." I surprised myself at the loudness of my voice, but sometimes Sun shut the door on things without even looking. "I don't know; why couldn't she at least talk to him for a minute?"

"Hay-den, she's past it. She knows who her father is; it's done. You always try to pick up lost causes; this one is lost for good."

"Yeah, well, that's just great, write off a guy for nothing, that you don't even know. At least Leg, uh, Mr. Reed doesn't go jerking off while looking into a mirror. Now *that's* an asshole!"

There was silence. Maybe twenty second's worth, but it sounded like an hour.

"Well," Sun said, in a sharp but low voice, "Steve's not in the picture anymore. Because he is an asshole. But not for anything you know about. And you're an asshole too! Thanks for reminding me!"

I didn't know that the sound of someone slamming down the phone could have a physical effect, but this one did. It was like Sun hammered a board into my ear. I put the phone back into the receiver and stretched my jaw open, because it felt like my ears were popping, like when an airplane descends.

Sun and I had reconnected all right. But like one of those magnetic connections, where when one of the connected magnets is turned around, the connection pops to the repulsion side. Antimagnetic charm, that's me. But she did say old Handyman Steve was out of the picture. That has to be good, right? Maybe not good for me in particular, but I don't need to dwell on that now. Now it's time to get ready for work.

Even though it was early December, I was still walking to work, unless it was pouring. San Francisco can have pretty temperate winters, and today was cool, but semi-sunny. I was late, so I didn't have any breakfast. No sign of Drew. He'd recovered, sort of, from the pneumonia, but he'd dropped some weight, which didn't look particularly good on his already narrow frame. Still coughing all the time. He had been claiming that the docs had said he was fine, until he admitted that he had only seen a doctor once. I hadn't seen him for almost a week, but that wasn't all that unusual, since he'd get shacked up with some new boyfriend every once in a while, and it went hot and heavy until it didn't, and then he'd come home. I figured that was what was up.

As for Roland, I saw him going out of the bathroom about three days ago and he even said "Hey" to me. And he'd bought some house groceries last week. Guy's almost human.

When I got near the old Woolworth's building on Market, I saw Leg Man talking to the Prophet. I was on the other side of the street, so I stopped and watched for a bit. The Prophet is a home-less guy too, a huge guy with a huge white beard, though I don't think he's nearly as old as Leg Man. I called him the Prophet because he looks like he might have come down from the heavens in a flaming chariot. But without bathing afterwards. His deal is that he just sticks his hand out at people on the street, doesn't say anything, pretty much doesn't look at them, and waits for them to give him dough.

I've walked by him a bunch of times but I've never heard him talk. I've nodded to him a few times when I thought he might be looking at me, but nothing. I'm surprised he ever gets anything from anybody—his hands are these giant, meaty things, and not real clean; he's almost scary. But today I see him talking to Leg Man. Figures—they must all know one another. Maybe they picnic together.

I started to walk on, but then reconsidered. Maybe if I dropped a message to Leg Man about his daughter—and I would leave the "asshole" part out—I can at least take that delivery service to Megan to get some kind of points. What the hell. So I walked up to them.

The Prophet was facing the street, against the building, with Leg Man's back to me. It was weird, because when I came up behind Leg Man, the Prophet moved toward me without saying anything, and I stopped moving altogether. A giant bearded guy will do that to you.

"Uh, Mr. Reed? Hello. Remember me, Hayden? I drove you back from UC Santa Cruz that day?"

The Prophet had moved almost in front of Leg Man, but Leg Man turned fully around, saw me, and came forward. "Hayden, right. Hayden, this is Sully."

The Prophet stepped forward and said in a deep voice, "Hayden." He nodded and extended his hand. He gave my hand a quick shake, which was like a having a briefcase open and close on my little paw, but with an oddly gentle touch.

"What can I do for you Hayden?" said Leg Man.

"Well, it's kind of confusing, but I was the connection for your daughter. I mean, I know the woman in Santa Cruz who was supposed to connect with your daughter. Through Megan. Megan doesn't know her though."

Leg Man walked a little closer to me, and cocked his head. "What kind of shit are you telling me? You're involved with Tabby too? What are you people doing?" He cleared his throat and spit a large glob of sputum on the sidewalk, not all that far from my shoe.

"No, not me. I mean, I don't know her. I saw her that day in the coffee shop. See, my old girlfriend knows her. Not really knows her, though, not before us all being in the coffee shop."

The Prophet laughed, a low, rolling rumbling sound. "So these are your new best friends you were telling me about, Jacob. Quite a crew. Don't know if they could find their rears with a compass," he said.

Leg Man glared at the Prophet, and turned back to me. "Any chance you could wash off the mud of what you just said? 'Cause it's coming through loud and stupid," he said.

I moved a little distance from the glob of spit. "Sorry. See, I think you know Megan's my boss. She asked me to ask my old girlfriend, Sun, who lives in Santa Cruz, to ask Tabitha about maybe getting together with you. Megan was just trying to help." The last sentence came out in a quivery voice, with a little lift at the end, like I was asking a question. One I shouldn't have asked.

"Help!" Leg Man shouted. "Did I *ask* for any help? Are you and Megan now my helpers? What the fuck?" He turned to the Prophet and threw his hands up in the air, and then turned back to me. "Look," he said, his voice calmer but still loud, "what goes on between my daughter and me is our business. That's a flat fact. Nobody helpin' things here, particularly no strangers. You people are probably all right, but maybe not, but that's no difference—nobody is going to help me with my daughter. Got it?"

I nodded, perhaps ten times. "Right," I said. "I understand. Well, it's time to get to work. I'll see you." I nodded to the Prophet, who looked at me without a response. When I'd walked about two steps, he let go of that low, rumbling laugh again. Somehow I knew that Leg Man hadn't quickly told him a joke.

Even with my foot in my mouth, I was still able to walk up Market to Consolidated. Pretty much all of the earthquake debris had been cleaned up, but there were still a few buildings that were closed, a couple of them red-tagged. I had noticed a few mom and pops that looked like they were shut down completely, now half-empty, the corner-liquor kinds of places that maybe the owners had had for a couple of generations. The land rolls the dice; some people come up with snake eyes.

I sat in my cube for a bit, half-heartedly looking at a contract for leasing a bunch of backhoes to some kind of property developer in the Central Valley. Make that quarter-heartedly. Consolidated had jumped right back into the post-quake swing of things, lawyers lawyering, vice-presidents vice-presidenting, crushingly bored proof-reading managers wishing for another earthquake. I thought I'd talk to Megan about Tabitha; she could use the update.

Megan was standing behind her desk, facing away from the door, putting a folder or an envelope high up on a shelf. She was wearing an uncharacteristically tight maroon skirt, and it hiked up a bit up toward her butt. I paused for a second and took that in, remembering the night at her apartment. But you know how they say sometimes things from your past flash in front of you out of the blue? The blue moment I instantly remembered was Casbah Megan falling asleep on the Couch of Iniquity, with Lothario the Loser sort of in her arms. I was so deep in that pretty picture that it startled me when she turned around.

"Hayden, what are you doing? Why didn't you knock or say something?"

"Uhh, I was just thinking of something, and I was out of it for a sec. Hey, can we talk for a moment?"

She looked at me, and then gestured for me to close the door. I pulled forward one of the extra chairs so it was in front of her desk, and we both sat.

"Listen, I talked to that Reed guy about his daughter, but it didn't go very well."

She opened her eyes wide and parted her lips as though she was going to speak, but she said nothing. I waited a moment and continued.

"Yeah, so I'd heard back from Sun, my friend in Santa Cruz that his daughter really didn't want anything to do with him. I guess Sun has been hanging out with her sometimes. Anyway, on the way to work today, I saw him talking to this other homeless guy I see all the time, and I went up to tell him."

Megan had closed her mouth, and was leaning, both hands palm down on her desk, toward me, but she still didn't speak. I waited for a blink, which didn't come, and then went on.

"OK, the thing is that I hadn't even got to the part about what his daughter—"

When Jacob Reed opened the door of Megan's office, my back was to him, so I couldn't see him. What I could see was that Megan drew back from her desk as though she was yanked with a rope, and her eyes were popping. But I could hear very well: before I fully saw Leg Man, he'd slammed a book down on Megan's desk hard enough to make her pen cup jump off the desk onto the ground, spilling a bunch of pens and pencils.

"Your Bronte!" he shouted. He was now alongside of me in front of the desk, the veins on his neck bulging like they'd explode. "Heathcliff and Cathy died—good riddance!"

I'd asked for an earthquake, and I'd gotten one. I could hear some murmur of voices outside the office, and a little commotion. Megan stood up, face drained, shaking slightly.

"Jacob, Mr. Reed, there's no need ... Please, please sit." The words came out like little frogs that hadn't quite learned to jump yet. She gestured oddly with her arm toward one of the other chairs, but it looked more like a spasm than a helping indicator. I hadn't moved, except to crane my neck to take it all in.

"Nobody's going to sit! No sitting. Here's how it is: you got your book, you got your clean little office and your clean little job and your little valet here—keep 'em. What you don't have is me! I'm walking out of here, and there's no need to ever trouble me or my family again."

He stood, glaring, waiting for Megan to speak. She took a deep breath, and probably would have said something pointedly neutral, in some classic, now-composed Meganesque way, but she was interrupted by two building security people and an actual city cop. Oh boy.

I was grateful, no, almost beholden to the gods, that Leg Man didn't resist the cop during the arrest. He acted as though it had happened a hundred times, and maybe it had. The real cop cuffed him, read him his rights, and they took him out, with pretty much the entire office crowding the aisle or looking over their cubicle walls. Megan vehemently protested the arrest—"He hasn't done anything! Stop!"—even taking the cop's name and badge number, which I thought was a little brave, since McManus was hanging out with his full vice-president's girth right in the doorway. I figured McManus had called it in, but I didn't ask.

But after they took Leg Man away, McManus asked me to leave the office, and he shut the door to talk to Megan alone. I gave her a little wave when I left, but she didn't offer a response. She sat at her desk, looking grimly ahead, and McManus sat in my chair, and they went through a little theatrical production of remonstrance and resistance. Or something like that. I didn't know much about the theatre, but I knew this was a play I'd rather not attend.

TWENTY ONE

....

This was one glad man when he got home. That man being me, and gladder yet that there was beer in the refrigerator. I thought about opening the entire six-pack at once and drinking it out of a bucket, but because I have impeccable manners, I refrained. I flopped onto the big living room couch, where because I was so splayed out, the biggest mirror ball on the coffee table showed me to have distortedly giant legs and a bit of a praying mantis head. Pretty accurate for today, I'd say.

I looked muzzily around for a while before I noticed the flowers on the mantle above the non-working fireplace. The display was stunning, particularly for it being the edge of winter—a spray of colors, sunflowers and wild skinny twiggy things, and what were probably lilies, a few roses and some bronzy leafy stuff I didn't know the name of. Pretty nice.

Wait—flowers? Drew's home. I got up and looked down the hall, and saw that his door was closed. His door was probably the most psychedelically painted thing in the house, a Grateful Dead poster gone to the Spiral Nebula and back, and because Drew had made his own stencil set of letters he'd designed, he put a bunch of funny words—"Pachyderm" and "Rhomboid" and more—in various sizes, colors and angles on the door as well. It was good crazy.

I went to the door and listened for a moment. Nothing. Nothing of course from Roland's room, because he'd literally draped heavy quilts on all the walls and even the door, because of his sound editing for his weird film stuff. At least that's what he said. I think he would have worn one of the quilts over his head and gone to work that way if they'd let him.

I thought maybe I shouldn't wake Drew if he'd been sleeping, since he'd been pretty sick, but he'd been gone a week on some fling or something, so he must be better. I knocked.

"Yeah." His voice was pretty garbled, but he sounded like he was awake.

"Hey man, it's Hayden. Haven't seen you for a bit. You feeling better?"

There was a long pause, and I was a second away from apologizing and backing off, but then he said, "Hayden. Yeah. C'mon in."

Drew's room was always a nightmare. Don't believe all that crap about gay guys being ever-so-tidy and all. He usually had clothes all over the place, dishes, old flower arrangements, whatever. But this was Drew-in-the-cave: awful mess, with crumpled-up papers, towels and crap everywhere, floor and bed, and it smelled like he hadn't showered in a week. But that was me glancing at the room before I looked at him. He shocked me.

He'd dropped a lot of weight. A lot. He was propped up in bed with a few big pillows behind him, covers up to his waist, and he was wearing a dirty white tank-top t-shirt. He had some mottled, raised bruises on his face, a couple of small ones on his cheeks and a big one on his forehead, purple and bluish and awful. It looked like there was one on his forearm too.

"Drew, what the fuck? Did you get into a fight at the bar? You look like shit!"

He was wearing the weird black half-glasses he sometimes wore, which he kept on a chain around his neck when he used them, mostly when he was messing with his typography stencils. He called them his "Princess Rita wear." He took them off before he spoke.

"You're only as pretty as you feel, Hayden. And I'm not feeling very pretty." He adjusted the pillows from behind and grimaced. "Sit down. I'm glad you came in. I wanted to talk to you."

He patted the only corner of the bed that wasn't covered with stuff, and I sat. When I looked back up at him, from this closer distance, I saw that his eyes were startlingly bloodshot. The bruises were bizarre, like blisters almost, maybe filled with fluid.

Drew looked at me for a moment, and smiled a little. "Pretty bad, huh? I can't believe it when I look in the mirror either. Not really a prime boy toy right now." He set down a sheaf of what almost looked like contracts from Consolidated and leaned back. "So, I'll give you the good news and the bad news. The bad news is that there is no good news. The rest of the news is that I'm sick. Pretty sick."

His voice wavered a little, and he took a sharp intake of breath, followed by another. "Hayden, I'm sorry to bring this to you like this, but I'm real sick. I have AIDS."

I rose a little and sat back down, and made a noise that sounded like "Urrhh." I was aware of AIDS; I lived in San Francisco, how could I not be? It had been killing people all over the country, by the thousands, in waves. They had very recently figured out that it was spread by sex and blood contact, so people had started to calm down—at least in the City—about the paranoia that it was spreading on toilet seats, gay waiters touching food, through the very air. But of course large swaths of the population still believed pretty much anything about homosexuals and their filthy ways. You could read about that shit every day. Hell, they were quarantining gay people in Cuba. Look what we did with the Japanese in World War II.

"Aww, Drew, man that's, that's so crappy. That is, oh—hey, I'm really sorry. That's just hell."

He was crying but smiling too. "I guess I'm going to pay for all my play, right? God's revenge and all. The weird thing is that I've always thought God and I had a pretty good deal going."

I didn't say anything, and for a moment, neither did he. But then he picked up the papers he'd been holding and said, "You wouldn't believe what I'm signing here. It's almost funny how many papers you have to sign when you're going to die."

When he said "die," he really started crying, the kind of big, shuddering sobs that a little kid who's bumped his head makes, but this kid wasn't going to come back from his bump. I moved up slightly on the bed and kind of grabbed his foot, or really, one of his big toes through the covers.

"Ahh, Drew, it's just so lousy, it's so shitty. I'm so sorry man."

He stopped crying, and wiped at his eyes with his hand. "It is what it is. It's OK. I've had a crazy time. I regret some stuff I've done, but mostly it's been a good ride. So, anyway, this paperwork: I'm actually going to go into a hospice, right down the block. Is that crazy?" He laughed and gestured with the papers east, down toward the freeway. "Yeah, I can walk down in my pajamas. But I'm going to check in,"—here he did that "air quotes" gesture—"in a week or so, and you don't check out. You'll have to find another housemate."

"C'mon Drew. We don't even have to think about that now. You're going to be around for a while." I looked off at a shelf above his head, which had a bunch of little stuffed animals on it; I'd never noticed that one was a weird Minnie Mouse in a leather miniskirt. "Maybe you'll even get better ..."

Neither of us said anything for a moment. Then he looked at me and said, "It's OK, Hayden. Nobody's getting better, but we don't have to talk about this stuff right now. One thing though—

I'm going to throw a little party on Saturday, so you'd better wear your best dress." He laughed, and then nodded at me with a small smile.

"OK," I said. I was the one starting to cry now. I got up and walked out, shutting the door so softly I could have been a burglar. I walked back to the living room, back to my beer, back to the mirror ball that showed my distorted face, a mask of grimness. Maybe not so distorted after all.

Drew hadn't even hit thirty-five yet. I remembered the first time I'd eaten dinner with him at the house, him and a friend of his, a pretty woman with crazy dyed electric-red hair, and I'd thought it might be his girlfriend at first. He'd made spaghetti, and he kept tossing single strands from the boiling pasta up to the high kitchen ceiling, and though they all stuck, he kept saying, "Not done yet!" and he'd throw another. He and the woman kept laughing, both of them with these fluttery high laughs, and I thought again that he might be gay or bi or something else. But I liked him, I liked him flinging the spaghetti, and laughing his girly laugh. I liked him so much more now. I couldn't imagine him dying—as weird as he was, he was probably my sanest friend in the City.

I didn't want another housemate. Drew was the guy who ran the house, held it together. Things since the quake had been nuts; I'd been happy to come back home and have it seem normal. But it was clear there really was no normal.

TWENTY TWO

···

J acob had been in jail before. He'd popped some guy in a bar in the Tenderloin years ago who'd said to his face, just a couple of months after he'd come back from his tour, that "Vietnam vets are pussies." One shot to the jaw and the clown was out. The guy had some meat-grinder lawyer brother who wanted to press assault charges, but they'd dropped the case even before it began. The last time was for a drunk and disorderly, years ago, one of the last times he'd really tied one on before he went cold sober. He'd done three and a half days in the San Bruno jail because the one on Bryant in the City was full and the court calendar was jammed.

This time it was pretty quiet on Bryant. And cold. They give you some kind of Army-issue blanket, the same scratchy, dull-green wool that he'd seen in bases all over. One blanket, that's it. Along with a lumpy mattress that can't be more than two inches high, bobbling on its creaky springs. He'd been in a four-bunk cell before, but this was a two, and his cellmate was a young Hispanic guy who didn't seem to speak much English. He gave Jacob a tight smile from the top bunk after he'd arrived that morning, said his name was Hector, and then turned over and went back to sleep.

Man, I wish I could sleep like that guy, thought Jacob. *Tired, real tired. Guess I was a little loud when I returned that book to Megan. Shit. Everyone's a librarian now. Make a little noise, go to jail. What if someone gets into my cabinet while I'm in here?*

He wasn't going to go before the judge for a preliminary hearing until tomorrow. Jacob could have called a bail bondsman and easily paid for his temporary release, but he didn't think it was worth it. He could sleep in a cold cell as well as anybody; he'd seen much colder nights, and much dirtier bedding. And he had his main money stash in the duffel they'd confiscated at the station, so if someone wanted to steal the rest of his shit from the alley, let 'em. He was just settling into his bunk when the cop that had locked him in opened the cell door.

"OK Reed, up and at 'em. You're out on bond."

Jacob swung his legs off the bunk to the floor, and leaned forward so that he could push his head out from under the top bunk. "I didn't pay any bond. What are you talking about?" Jacob said.

The officer glanced at a clipboard. "Woman out front paid your bond. Little blond named Thornstock. Get up and let's go."

"Shit," Jacob said.

It took twenty minutes to go through processing, with Jacob signing the documents promising to appear the next day, and receiving his duffel bag back. But when he exited the processing hall and entered the jail's main entry area, Megan was sitting on a concrete bench, along with an older couple. She stood up when he came into the room.

"Jacob, I'm so sorry about what happened at the office. I had nothing to do with the police being called."

Jacob stopped about ten feet from Megan, and smiled, with his lips tight. "So, I get it now. You one of those guardian angels. Kind of like that Clarence guy in *It's a Wonderful Life,* right? You swoop in and toss things around and make it all crazy, no matter if the guy needs a guardian angel or not." He shook his head and smiled the flat-lipped smile again. "Just figures I'd get a white, suit-wearing guardian angel from downtown. I guess that's God's sense of humor."

Megan moved a little closer to Jacob and said softly, "Jacob, I know it seems as if I've been interfering, and I apologize for that. But you must know that—"

Jacob slung the big duffel over his shoulder and shook his hand in the air several times. "Nope, don't need to know. Really don't. All I know is that I'm heading back over to the building and that I'm probably heading to another part of town to do my business after that. I appreciate you putting up the bail money, and I'll drop the repayment off at your office tomorrow, if they don't arrest me."

He nodded to Megan and headed to the door.

"But Mr. Reed—Jacob, I have to go back to work too. We can ride the same Muni car back together."

Jacob didn't turn around, but waved his hand in the air again as he continued walking. He opened the glass door and said loudly, without turning back to Megan, "Plenty of Muni cars to come. No need to crowd up on the seats together. You have a nice life, Megan."

Though late afternoon, it was warmer outdoors than it had been in the cell, though there was a breeze. He started up Bryant and a piece of paper lifted off the sidewalk and curled around his shin. He picked it off and saw it was a handwritten letter. He stopped for a moment and looked it over. It was from a man named Helcomb or Hilamb or something strange like that, to a woman named Rebecca. Something about a piece of furniture that one of them had and the other wanted. Jacob continued walking, and tossed the letter into a trashcan. *Maybe Tabby would listen to me if I wrote her a letter. Nothing complicated or crybaby, just tell her how it's been for the past few years, how it's different now. How it's better. And that I miss her. Couldn't make it any worse.* He quickened his pace and whistled a little tune as he headed to the Muni stop.

TWENTY THREE

··

Drew was pretty out of it all day Saturday, but late in the afternoon, he got up and asked me to help decorate for the party. I'd spent most of the day in my room, working on the novel. I'd had a bit of a breakthrough: the media mogul *Karamozov*-inspired dad is indeed kidnapped by his family, but there's a twist. He's a bastard for sure, but they've had him kidnapped to protect him from Mafioso types who want to strong-arm his media empire and channel its cash their way. But the coke-jonesing daughter, who is the only one who has actual contact with the kidnappers, goes into a drug-coma. It turns out that the kidnappers don't really know the kidnapping is for protection of dad, and coke-for-brains can't tell them to take it easy on their dad or tell her brothers how to contact them, because she's unconscious. And the Mafia's closing in too.

Might sound like too much of a detective caper, but I've added a bunch of family dynamics and psychosocial layers. I'm going to parallel *Karmazov's* Grand Inquisitor section later with a long courtroom scene, with the judge going back and forth with the family's lawyer on issues of God and free will. That part's kind of a mess now, but I can work with it.

Drew's ideas of decorating for a party were a bit different than mine. I've always thought that the best decoration for a party was lots of beer, with maybe some vodka in the wings. And chips, plenty of chips. But Drew hung these long paisley silk scarves across the mantle and over some of the lamps. Then he took these big stuffed-animal Disney characters he had in his room—Mickey and Minnie and Pluto and Goofy—and put the kind of black masks like what Zorro wore in that old TV show on them. And then added bikinis. I don't know why he had a bunch of bikinis that would fit stuffed Disney characters, but he did. He placed them in various spots in the living room.

Then we both hung long ribbons of colored crepe paper across the living room to the dining room, and he taped a bunch of white envelopes to the crepe paper that had a single word on them, like "Sexy," and "Intrigue" and "Desperate." Inside the envelopes he'd put a small toy or fortune cookie or weird photograph. In the centerpiece of the big living room coffee table, the one with the mirror balls, he put a huge bong that was shaped like a cock. You loaded the pot into a scooped-out area on the bong's balls, and you sucked the very-realistic looking (but huge) head of the bong-cock to get high. I thought that I'd probably just drink.

I already regretted inviting Sylvie and Crenshaw to the party. Not that they weren't fun, but that neither of them had ever been to a gay party before. I'd made the mistake of talking about it to

Sylvie yesterday, and she'd piped up with "That sounds great! Can I come?" and immediately Crenshaw had popped his head out from his cube and asked, "Me too?" I'd said yes before I'd even considered it, and later thought that it would be more fun for me if some of my friends were there too. But I don't think I'd sufficiently warned them that some of Drew's friends were pretty crazy. My mistake.

After we finished with the crepe, he went back to bed to rest. He looked like hell, though he'd done a decent job of covering up—with makeup—the lesions on his face and on one of his arms, which I'd found out were called Kaposi's sarcomas. You could still see the big lumps, but they weren't the fiery purple and blue that they were without the makeup. He was coughing badly, the kind where your whole body—and he didn't have much body left—shakes.

The kitchen was trashed, so I cleaned it up. Drew had spent a lot of Friday making a huge batch of fancy appetizer things, artsy little crackers with stuff like asparagus and tiny onions and olives and a lot of spreads and dips, hummus and chutneys and sliced bell peppers and cheeses. He'd also laid out a bunch of good booze, Jack Daniel's and Stoli and more. We were ready for the onslaught.

And that began around eight.

I opened the door to the Stardust Twins, Rhonda and Donda. Since I'd met Rhonda and Donda a couple of times, I wasn't that surprised by their outfits, but I have to say they were inventive. They were both wearing lime-green suede leather miniskirts, with long cowboy-style fringes. Both of them were wearing electric purple shirts, probably silk. They both had silver six-shooters with holsters, covered with jewels, naturally. The final touch was the literal topper: they each wore, well up on the sides of their heads, those tiny bowler-style hats like you see high-in-the-Andes Peruvian village women in *National Geographic*.

Maybe this goes without saying, but Rhonda and Donda were guys, and they weren't really twins. Rhonda was Puerto Rican and Donda was white. Rhonda was the talkative one, and he gave me a hug and said, "Now Hayden, don't you touch my hair! I know you want to, but I'm saving it for marriage." Both of the twins had longish black hair, though I think Donda's was dyed. They had both sprayed on some high gloss for the occasion. Donda swirled by me and into the living room, giving my cheek a soft touch as he went by.

Drew had been playing some kind of opera before anyone arrived, telling me that I had to stand it because he was dying. Funny guy. He knew I hated opera, but he had mercy after the Stardust girls came over, and put on some kind of house/electronica stuff that was slightly more tolerable. Rhonda's voice immediately rose over the loud music.

Drew was looking pretty tame in relation to what he normally wore for one of his parties. He had on tight black shiny pants, a tight sleeveless t-shirt that really showed his lost weight, and a lavender snood-like thing that wrapped up his hair almost like a turban. And one long, dangly hoop earring. I watched him talk to Rhonda and Donda. He was laughing and smiling, but his voice was pretty weak. But he was obviously happy. Everyone who was coming over knew the drill, that he was down for the count. Except for Silvie and Crenshaw, who didn't need to know.

And neither did Diana, who shocked me by being at the door when I answered the bell. I couldn't even sputter out a hello, giving her my best deer-in-the-headlights look. "Hayden, hey, what's happening? Silvie told me about your party, and how to get here. I love the colors of the walls!"

She leaned in to me on the step, and gave me a quick kiss on the cheek. She smelled very, very good, sort of like a floral pastrami sandwich. Or something like that. I would have given her a kiss back, except for the hulking stooge standing behind her, who had his arm halfway around her waist.

"Hayden, this is my friend Mario. Mario, Hayden." So Mario gives me the manly grip and the 300-watt smile. He goes about six-three, maybe 200, thick, dark wavy hair, looks and dresses like a clothing ad model—expensive clothing, by my guess—and seems genuinely happy to be alive. I hate him, but I let him in.

By this point, there were twenty or so people in the joint, and it was pretty loud. When Drew drinks, his high laugh gets even higher, and I heard it a few times, but it was always followed by a coughing fit. At one point, he had to go back to his room for a while because the coughing nearly knocked him out.

Around eleven, two of the party stars appeared. One was a guy that I didn't know, dressed in a black leather vest and tight black leather shorts with a prominent pink codpiece leading the way. He wasn't that unusual for a pal of Drew's, except that he had a dog leash on a friend, who was on all fours (with gloves and kneepads), wearing what looked to be a latex or rubber suit that was electric yellow. He was led around on all fours because Codpiece Man had him leashed to a tight, studded dog collar. I didn't know Rubber Rover either, but everyone else seemed to know them both, especially when Codpiece produced a bunch of whippets out of his little leather fanny pack and gathered a small crowd around when they started huffing the little cartridges.

All that was fine with me, except that Mario and Diana seemed to be more than just pals. Those two had been mostly talking with Sylvie and Crenshaw, though they'd more than mingled with Drew's crowd. I'd seen Sylvie doing tequila shots with a guy in a baby-blue Spandex bicycling outfit, and they were laughing so hard they were crying. Mario was laughing his head off as well, though at one point he seemed a bit unbalanced around Rover, who had pretended to sniff well up his leg into his manly Mario-ness. But Mario just backed up behind Diana and smirked a bit.

Of course, all of the boys in the band loved Mario; they couldn't stop crowding around, some of them pinching his cheek. Diana took that all in, though when Mario had a crowd of men around him, she pulled him away with a mean little laugh. I kept glancing at Diana, hoping she'd throw a look my way, but it didn't happen. None of the girls or boys could touch her in shortness of skirt; the soft, velvet-like red mini she was wearing would have made a fine hat, for what it covered of Diana's long legs—and other fine attributes. Nope, no one could touch her, and after watching her and Mario cavorting around the party, I could see that I wouldn't be doing any touching either.

My favorite party moment was when Roland came out of his room with one of his movie cameras, and did a full, slow panorama of the living room and the kitchen, with all of its dramatic denizens. He was finishing up his pan in the hall when the camera stopped, lingering on Diana, moving up and down her willowy frame. It took a moment, but she spotted Roland, gaped at him and then said, "Get lost, creep!" That sent him scurrying back to his room, without a word.

Somewhere around one, a clump of the partygoers were trying to collectively sing "Bohemian Rhapsody," led by Crenshaw, who had one of his arms around Donda and one around a woman with a shaved head and a Maori-like tattoo up one side of her face. Crenshaw was dead drunk, and was making up for his lack of memory of the lyrics with increased amplitude, so that his cheeks were flaming red with every chorus. They were just getting to Scaramouch's fandango when Crenshaw let loose with a tide of colorful vomit into the center of the room. Lucky we had hardwood floors.

That pretty much put the finishing touch on the party. Sylvie cleaned up Crenshaw, who rallied a bit afterward, offering to go into "We Will Rock You," but nobody took him up on it. People started straggling out, and Codpiece came up to me and said, "One for the ages, really," and kissed me on the cheek. His bristly unshaven face almost woke me from the haze I was in, but when he said, "Give my best to Drew," I jumped; I realized that I hadn't seen him for more than an hour. I went back to his room, which had the door closed. I knocked softly, but there was no response. Probably exhausted, and why wouldn't he be?

Diana and Mario were one of the last couples to leave, along with Codpiece and Rubber Rover. Mario gave me a friendly clap on the back and told me I really knew how to throw a party. Diana, who was probably an ounce less drunk than me, put both of her hands on my shoulders, and being that she was wearing giant high heels, looked directly into my eyes and said, "This was really great Hayden. I've never been to a queer party before. It's really great to get to know your friends, and to see how you guys all get along.

They're all so funny, like you." She kissed me on the end of my nose, and they both left.

So, there you have it. The babe I'd been trying to work for months now thought I was a three-dollar bill. It was funny, all right. What was even funnier was that I found one of Rover's yellow knee-pads in the refrigerator when I was putting some stuff away. That was funny, but there was no one around to share the joke with, so I just put it on the kitchen table and went to bed.

TWENTY FOUR

....

Jacob had been in the phone booth for more than fifteen minutes; he hadn't picked up the receiver. He'd deliberately walked to the sleaziest phone booth in the neighborhood, the one on the corner of Sixth and Market. The door glass was completely broken through in one section, so that the broken edge of a pane protruded a little into the booth. There were balls of crumpled trash on the floor, as well as what looked to be a small patch of old vomit. A stain that was probably blood adorned the small shelf provided in the booth to write notes. The empty chain that once held the phonebook hung limply on the wall. Jacob wanted a reminder of where he was, so that he could think from that, to where he'd like to be.

He shifted again on his feet in the booth, this time looking down Sixth. A very tall, skinny black man wearing a porkpie hat walked toward the booth with a boom box on his shoulder, jouncing to the music that blared out of the box. He nearly collided with a UPS delivery driver who had double-parked to run into a liquor store near the corner. A homeless woman, her age hidden in multiple layers of ragged clothing, the knit cap pulled low over her face and the deeply creased tan that only comes from endless days on the street, leaned against one side of the booth looking up Market, holding a sign that matched her weather-beaten look. The sign in big black letters simply read, "Help." Nearest to Jacob on the sidewalk, amid the continually changing crowd of passersby was a young man, maybe in his thirties, with long, ragged, brilliantly red hair who was drinking a yellowish-colored wine from a bottle, and singing an incoherent song.

Jacob watched the man drink and sing. *T-bird,* he thought. *That stuff will kick you in the gut harder than a slug from an M-16. Guy probably started out with brown hair and's been drinking Bird for the past month and it burnt his hair. Shit.* He turned back to the phone, cleared his throat, and lifted the receiver. He'd looked at the phone number written on the scrap of paper so many times he didn't have to look again when he dialed.

"Hello?"

"Tabby, is that you?"

There was a long pause, and Jacob could hear an intake of breath.

"Yes, it's me. How did you get this number?"

"Well, bit of a story. You probably didn't notice those white folks that were sitting near us when we were talking at the school café. Well, those folks—"

It was clear that Tabitha was trying to deflect the irritation in her voice, but the deflection was only partial. "Yeah, right. Listen, I know about those people. Sun's old boyfriend. She told me about him, and the other woman. What about them?"

"Well, you know, they somehow got in the middle of things here, and they don't belong. They're just people I happened to meet. They aren't family."

There was a longer pause. "Sun's a close friend. Closer than some family. What's this about?"

Jacob looked out of the booth. The red-haired drunk was almost finished with the wine, and was doing a series of small jig-like steps in a circle around another ragged man with a huge birthmark on his face who was sitting in the middle of the sidewalk. Jacob turned back to the telephone.

"Well, we didn't really finish our conversation. And you didn't answer the letter I sent ten days ago. I mean, I'm not trying to make you feel bad, I just thought we could talk a bit more. And there's no need for any of these other folk to be a part of that."

"A part of what?" There was a sharper edge to Tabitha's voice. "What is this thing that has any parts anyway, what are you talking about? There's you basically getting blind-ass drunk for years, and then leaving mom. Leaving us. Aren't those the parts?"

The tear left Jacob's cheek so quickly he didn't have time to wipe it. It landed near the vomit stain, and was followed by another. He hadn't cried in years; producing the two tears surprised him, but the shakiness of his voice when he responded surprised him more.

"Tabby, that's how it was. That's how it *was*, but that isn't now. I haven't had a drink in five years. Five years! I've saved some money." The words had shuddered out, thin and poorly pronounced. He took in a big breath and expelled it slowly. "Listen, how's your brother, how's Joshua? Your mom won't tell me anything about him. How is he?"

"He's OK. Taller." She laughed a little. He asked me for a motorcycle for his birthday." Her tone turned dark. "You remember his birthday, right? He's going to be fifteen. "I remember," Jacob said softly. "I've sent some cards for years, for you too, but your mother told me she never gave them to you or to Josh. I've never stopped thinking about you guys and—"

"Hey, get over it. What's done is done. Look dad, I'm not going to hang up on you, but I really don't think we have that much to talk about, so take care, OK?" She paused for a moment, and then softly hung up the phone.

Jacob continued to hold the phone to his ear; the dial tone didn't register in his hearing. *Josh, fifteen. Damn.* Outside the booth, the red-haired man was now sitting cross-legged on the ground, playing what might have been solitaire on the sidewalk with a mottled deck of cards. The woman who had been leaning against the phone booth was sitting in front of the cards, rocking slowly, as though she was being given a psychic reading.

Jacob slowly opened the door and started walking back up Market toward Consolidated. After the arrest, he'd left the alley, and had set up shop a short distance from Sully, even sleeping behind the parking lot shed of Sully's, and checking in with him a couple of times a day. But he felt restless on that part of Market, and thought that he might be cramping Sully's style a little. He even set up not far from where Dexter blew his sax, but Dexter came up with some crazy scheme of how he and Jacob could do a kind of musical panhandling act, and that was a brick wall as far as Jacob was concerned. Besides, hours of listening to Dexter attempt to play some of Coltrane's squawking, discordant stuff drove him crazy. Didn't he ever listen to Trane's blues?

So he was back behind Consolidated, for better or worse. He'd seen Megan hurrying in to the building a couple of times, but she hadn't looked his way. Hayden too, though he thought he'd caught Hayden quickly turning away when Jacob had spotted him leaving after work. No matter.

Jacob walked, head down. He stepped on a dirty *Chronicle* front page fluttering on the sidewalk, whose headline read, "Since the Earthquake: What's Changed?" He walked a little further. *What's changed?* he thought. *Still a bum. Bum with a bum leg. No change.* He walked further, almost bumping into a striking woman with a very short skirt, carrying a briefcase and wearing mirrored sunglasses. She said, "Excuse me, sir" when he angled by her.

Sir? Sounded like she meant it too. Well, I don't know everything about people. He stopped suddenly and rubbed his unshaven jaw. *Tabby called me dad. Called me a bum too, but she called me dad.* He started walking again, a bit more quickly, up Market Street.

TWENTY FIVE

....

On Sundays, Megan always went to church. But there was no vaulted ceiling, no candlelit nave, no hushed rustling in straight-backed pews. Her church was within the tight confines of a book's spine, the liturgy indeed the Word, but steadfastly that of eighteenth- or nineteenth-century novelists rather than any dead scrolls. She occasionally strayed into a Woolf or a Plath, and even dipped into a Margaret Atwood now and then, but those occasions she viewed as flights of fancy. When she needed comfort, sustenance and direction, there was the canon: Bronte, George Elliot, and Austen, and a host of lesser priestesses.

She took her Sundays seriously. If there were no Consolidated emergencies, no looming deadlines, no calls that could only be caught up on a weekend, she kept her briefcase snapped shut, her day planner silenced. Instead there was teeming life between the pages, old intrigues, slights, leaps of faith and hammerings of the heart. Megan would open her curtains wide in the morning and read for hours in bed, or move to the expansive living room, with its strong light and big views. The vagaries of San Francisco weather were no impediment to literature's siren song: rain, fog or sharp sun—all were welcome in the room, all played across the pages.

So when the phone rang, amplified from its spot on her heavy beside table at 8:45 am the Sunday after Hayden's party, she was strongly tempted not to answer it. She was propped up with her fluffiest pillows against the headboard of her big bed, the powder-blue satin comforter pulled up just under her breasts. She had a large cup of coffee in her favorite mug, which depicted one of Georgia O'Keeffe's luscious Canna flower images. She was about 70 pages in on a beautiful cloth-bound edition of Kate Chopin's *The Awakening*, a novel she'd read perhaps seven times, each time with renewed pleasure. When the phone rang, she set the book down on the comforter and sighed.

I won't, she thought. *I don't have to and I won't. It's probably a mistaken call anyway, at this time on Sunday morning.* She looked at the phone on the heavy bedside table and frowned. The answering machine caught it after four rings: *Hello. This is Megan Thornstock. I'm away ...* but no one left a message. She was just lifting the book back up from the covers when the phone rang again.

Damn. She snatched the receiver from its cradle and said, "Yes, this is Megan."

"Megan, it's mother. How are you?"

Megan held the phone away from her face, sighed and shifted in bed, inadvertently closing her book. "Mother. Hello. I'm doing fine, though I am actually catching up on some work at the moment. Is everything OK?"

"Well, can that job be so important that you can't relax on a Sunday? I've never understood most Americans, and their penchant for incessant work."

"Mother, I'm not required to work on a Sunday, nor a Saturday either. I was simply clearing out some paperwork issues, not digging an irrigation trench. We aren't all savages in the California workplace."

"Well, speaking of the California workplace, your father and I have decided to come out and spend some time with you. Since it's been two full years since you've been home, and Christmas is near, and you have shown little interest in some strong opportunities for you here, we feel it is necessary to travel to San Francisco to provide you with a reminder of your family."

Megan slumped down on the bed, so that only her head was up on the headboard, at a strong right angle to her body. She glanced at the empty highball glass from last night that was near the base of the phone. "Mother, I'm fully aware of my family and its members. But I'm curious: whose idea was it to come out to San Francisco? Yours or father's?"

"It was originally my idea, but your father instantly acceded. Despite his busy schedule. Your father's work is manifestly important—his firm and many, many students depend on him, as well as the faculty," she said.

She paused a moment. "You know, Megan, we've never quite understood what your position with a company that leases various objects to various other entities entails. It's never seemed to have anything to do with your lasting love of literature."

"Mother, there's really no need to address this again. My company provides a service that helps many businesses and helps the employees of many businesses. I'm good at my work and I'm recognized for it. That work allows me to live in a beautiful apartment in San Francisco, surrounded by the literature I love, which doesn't go neglected."

Megan pulled hard at the receiver's cord with her free arm, holding it out at arm's length so that it pulled the phone a little away from her head. She could hear her mother's voice as though from a small radio at crisp volume.

"Yes, yes Megan, the virtues of San Francisco notwithstanding, it still yet seems that you aren't fulfilling a true calling. But I suppose a mother's advice doesn't have the currency it once had ..."

Her mother trailed off a bit in a characteristic way that was intended to prompt soothing sounds from Megan. Instead, she sat sharply upright in the bed. "Probably true, mother. I wonder if I could speak to Father for a moment."

"Oh, well, yes. Wait a moment."

Megan took a deep breath. It had been at least two months since she'd spoken with her father. Her mother had been the voluble conduit of all her father's doings, and Megan had only so much space available for her mother's concerns. For her father, she had unfilled spaces.

"I'm sorry Megan. Your father is actually working on a complex brief right now and there's a spot of bother with it. However, he says he's very much looking forward to our visit."

Megan's nostrils flared. "Too busy yet again? That's an answer that's no answer!" Megan stood up from the bed, picked up the phone and moved to her bedroom window, which looked down Taylor to a large ornate apartment building. A very small old woman, quite hunched, all in black, walked slowly down the street.

"Mother, please tell father that this isn't the best of time for a visit. The earthquake disrupted a great deal of our contract work at Consolidated, and we are just now returning to normal. I will have several overtime workweeks coming for the foreseeable future. I'll let you know when I have more flexibility in my schedule."

"But Megan, surely you can take some time off from your work while we are there! We haven't seen you in quite a while, you know. Can't you discuss it with your superiors?"

"I'm sorry mother—it's simply out of the question right now. In fact, I'm late getting ready for a coffee shop meeting among the company executives that could only be squeezed in this morning, so I'm afraid I'll have to go. I'll be in touch soon."

She softly hung up the phone, returned it to the table and sat on the side of the bed. *Father isn't the only one who is busy,* she thought. She climbed back in bed and picked up the book. She read two paragraphs, returned to the first, went back a page and then read the second of the two paragraphs again. Then she set the book down. She dressed so quickly that the clash of the green sweatshirt with the pinkish satiny pants didn't settle on her. She was up on the roof without remembering climbing the stairs.

After the quake damage to her rose bed, she hadn't attempted to replace all the damaged varieties. She had shored up the one cracked side of the bed, put the trellis back up, and had planted a number of ornamental bushes, still green here at year's end. She'd only planted one new rose, a Father Christmas, which showed little promise now, more of a stark cane with a few pale green leaves. She put a finger into the soil at its base, and picked up the nearby watering can and gave it a cursory splash. She lifted the edges of some of the bushes along the periphery of the bed, but saw nothing worth fussing over. She was heading to the rooftop door when Tuttle opened it and walked up and out.

"Megan, well, howdy do! Isn't this a pleasant surprise! Getting after the roses again, are you? I never did plant that corn I mentioned, but I guess I could still sneak some in, if I were a sneakin' man."

"Mr. Turknot, hello. Well, I don't think the corn would grow too well up here anyway. I'm sorry, but I'm on my way down; lots of errands today."

"Oh no, don't mind me, I was just coming up for some air. Cooled down quite a bit in the last couple of weeks. Still don't think we'll get the Christmas snow I used to see in Des Moines though!" Tuttle threw back his head and laughed so that Megan could see several gold fillings.

""No, not likely," said Megan, and then she exited the roof. *Second mention of Christmas today,* she thought. *When is it? A bit less than two weeks.* She made her way back into her apartment and sat on the edge of the couch, hunched forward, head in the palms of her hands. *I hope I wasn't too hasty with Mother about Christmas. Two years it's been. But I'd never hear the end from her about moving back home. And father—it's just as likely he'd be fretting over his missed work the entire time.*

She threw on a coat and headed to the stairs. A crowded Muni ride later, she was walking on J.F. Kennedy drive with a throng of other Sunday revelers. The City had had the good sense to close Golden Gate Park to vehicular traffic on Sundays, but that sometimes only meant that you had a greater likelihood of being run over by a roller-blader than a bad driver. Many couples were out strolling arm-in-arm; bicyclists rolled by, sometimes ridden by spandex-suited bodies serious about their peddling tasks, sometimes by families of three and four, the children straggling up the rear on their little machines. A boom box on a blanket crunched out some loud punk music in the middle of a cluster of young men and women who betrayed no reaction to the discordant notes.

Megan spoke to no one, except to say "No, no, don't," to a ragged homeless man in Army fatigues who tried to put a limp rose in her hair. His, "You aren't so hot after all, bitch," fell on deaf ears. She paused to listen to a trumpet player in the tunnel near the Conservatory of Flowers play a long, sustained mournful note. The hundreds of windows in the magnificent old building shone dimly in the scattered sun. She walked up to the Conservatory, closed because of some minor damage from the quake, to see if she could see any of the rare orchids in the tropicals exhibit, but the windows were so steamed from the building's humidification that she could only see murky shapes. She sat down on the Conservatory's steps and watched a very tan young man, shirtless in the late fall cool, do a series of graceful pirouettes, acrobatic catches and flips with a hacky sack. She opened her purse, looked at the tiny bottle of vodka inside, and touched its top. Then she held it in her palm. She put it back, got up and started walking toward the Haight.

Even though it was cool outside, the walk from the park to the Irish pub on Geary and Masonic made her perspire. She sat at the bar, which though the walls were darkly paneled, was bright from the big windows that looked out onto the patio outside. There was only one other person on the dark stools, a thin, blonde young man with a very long neck who looked like he might be underage. He slumped, his half-full pint of beer partially concealed by his slack shoulders. He didn't look up at Megan, who sat seven or eight stools away.

The first vodka tonic she drank quickly. She was thirsty, and its coolness, despite the slight burn of the tonic, was pleasant. The ruddy-faced bartender merely nodded at her empty glass and she nodded back for number two. The second drink was gone in less time than the first.

The bartender turned from the counter, a towel and a beer mug in his hand. "Little dry today?" he said.

"Yes, I'd been walking in the park. I walked here from there and became a little overheated. Would you mind making me another?"

"Mind? Hey, I'm the man behind the counter, aren't I? Happy to set you up. Ronnie, you want anything?"

The long-necked man looked up, and Megan could see that he'd been crying. His glass was still half-full. He shook his head at the bartender and slumped back down again.

Megan stared at the crying man for a moment and then looked away from him when her drink was delivered. *That man's very upset,* she thought. *Maybe something to do with his family. He looks young enough to still live at home.*

She drank the drink in long sips, careful to wipe the corners of her mouth after each one. The glass held mostly ice when the bartender appeared directly in front of her. "Could I get you a little lunch to go with your drinks? You don't want to be walking too far without a little lunch in you." He smiled, his reddened face matched by his bloodshot eyes.

"Lunch, no. Is it lunchtime? Oh yes, yes, it is lunchtime. No, just one more drink will do. I won't be walking." The bartender looked into her eyes for a second and then nodded. Before he was fully turned back to the bar she said, "Well, maybe a few French fries, if they aren't too greasy."

He laughed and said, "We have the finest grease this side of the park. Fries will be out in a minute." He made her drink and set it in front of her.

She took a few sips of her drink, and looked again at the long-necked man, who didn't appear to have moved. *It's possible that he simply needs cheering,* she thought. *Maybe he's had an argument with his parents.* She set the drink down at stepped toward him, but when she was a few feet away, he looked up at her and grimaced, showing dingy teeth caught in a crooked scowl.

Megan tottered a bit and shifted her walk to appear as though she was going toward the open pay phone booth on the wall of the bar. She approached the phone and leaned against it, thinking, *So unpleasant. Such an unpleasant look on that man.* She set her purse on the little shelf beneath the phone and it opened so that her pocket address book was visible. *Hayden,* she thought. *I should call Hayden.*

"This is Hayden."

"Hayden. Well. Your voice sounds positively hoarse. Are you ill?"

"Megan? Is that you? What—"

"Now Hayden, I'd heard through that so-called grapevine, though one wonders what the word origin might be, that you'd had a large party last night. Now, there's full understanding of why one wouldn't invite their supervisor to a non-work-related party, but considering our recent history, one would think a courtesy invitation would have been in order. Not that I would have attended, mind you, but, oh!"

Megan had been leaning on the phone booth's shelf, and her elbow slipped off, causing her to lurch forward and drop the receiver, and to almost hit her head on the booth's sidewall.

"Megan? Megan? What's going on? Are you there?"

She could hear Hayden's tinny voice spiraling out of the receiver as it dangled from its cord in front of the booth. She snatched it up and clapped it to her head, with more force than she intended.

"I'm here, I'm here! Just a little trouble with this phone. Regardless, what I wan—"

"Megan, where *are* you? Are you OK?" Hayden's voice was very loud in her ears, and she shook her head a little.

"I'm in an establishment, well, a restaurant near Golden Gate Park. I'd stopped in here for some water after a long walk. But to return to the subject ..."

"Megan, look, I'm sorry about the party, but really, I knew you wouldn't come, so it was pointless to ask. I don't think you would have liked it anyway. But it sounds like maybe you should go home and get some rest."

Hayden cleared his throat and paused for a moment. "Do you want me to come and get you and drive you home?"

"No need, no need in the least. I'm fully versed in the public transportation systems. Though the cars could be cleaner, of course." She flipped her hair back over her shoulder and leaned heavily on the shelf. "But the party is only part of what I wanted to discuss, Hayden. What needs discussing is Jacob. I'm very worried about the situation with his daughter. I think we need to intervene."

"Megan! Are you insane? Do you remember what happened the last time we got in the way of those two? We got screamed at and Jacob went to jail. If we mess with them again, we'll probably all end up in jail, if not worse."

"Hayden, one minute, one minute please."

Megan set the receiver down and went to the bar to pick up the last of her drink. She glanced at the blonde-haired man as she went by, but he sat as before, hunched deep in his reverie.

"My concern is that Jacob will be lost forever to his daughter. I realize that our initial efforts weren't well thought-out, but I have some considered thoughts on the matter. Your friend in Santa Cruz could very well be the key."

"Sun? No, not Sun again in this!" Hayden's voice rang sharply in Megan's ear. She held the receiver a little away from her head and took a long drink from her glass. "... and it really isn't any of our business anyway."

"Hayden, *of course* it's our business. Fathers and daughters are everybody's business. Besides, we were there in that café when they had that first argument. We can close that door and open another, a better door." She took the last long pull on her drink and set the glass loudly on the shelf. "I'm sure Jacob and, well, what's her name, Thomasina, yes, I'm sure they will both thank us in the end."

Hayden didn't speak for a moment. "Tabitha. Her name is Tabitha. Megan, listen, this really isn't the time to discuss this. Maybe we can talk about it tomorrow at work. I've got to go now anyway, but really, you shouldn't even try to take the Muni home. Call a cab—it will be easier and quicker."

"A cabbie ain't shabby." She giggled and tapped her fingers on the phone's shelf. "Isn't that from some American popular song? But yes, we can discuss this at work. I don't have my day planner with me, but I believe my morning is open. And you know where the door is." She laughed loudly, and then covered her mouth with her hand.

She walked back to the bar and spoke to the bartender, who was looking at what seemed to be a recipe book. "Sir, I'd like a cabbie to go. That's my order." She smiled and patted the bar. "I'll be waiting outside." She started to walk out, and then turned to the blonde man and said, "Family issues can be very challenging. But don't ever let them get the better of you." Then she stepped out into the late afternoon sun.

TWENTY SIX

E ven though it was a Monday, I woke up feeling better. Sundays are usually one of my prime days, where the hours feel elastic and open. I could just as well go bike across the bridge or work on my novel or wander through North Beach, or just do whatever. But yesterday? Yesterday my hangover had a hangover.

I coffeed up, popped in the shower and then got ready for work. It was drizzling in the December fog, but not too windy, so I decided to do the Market walk up to work. When I'd showered, I saw that Drew's door was shut. Naturally, Roland's was too. But when I put my cup in the kitchen, and turned to go, I heard a weird sound.

It was a hissing kind of noise, like a gas was being squeezed in short sprays from a propane tank or a furnace. I actually thought it was our hall furnace on the fritz, but when I looked down the hall, I could see that Drew's door was slightly open. The sound was Drew.

I took a couple of steps down the hall. "Drew? Hey man, is that you?"

A spluttering, choking sound came from Drew's room. I opened his door and he was sitting on his bed, slumped over, feet on the ground. When I came in, he held up his head for a moment, and kind of wiggled a finger at me. Then his head fell forward again. A terrible sound came from his throat, a kind of catching, broken wheeze.

I walked to the bed and sat down next to him. "Drew, what's going on?"

He lifted his hand and wiggled his finger again, this time pointing vaguely to the door. "It's time," he rasped. "It's time now."

I was so sorry to know exactly what he meant. He'd told me a couple of weeks ago that he might not be able to make it to the hospice himself, and he'd asked if I'd could help out. It was crazy really—they would have come and picked him up, but he wanted to be the one to direct his arrival. Drew always wanted to arrange things, to check off the lists, to be the man behind the curtain.

The hospice was only a few blocks away. Lucky for me, he was already dressed, though I put on his warmest coat over his shoulders, what he called his "cowboy coat," a sheepskin/shearling thing that was heavy on the lining. He needed it, because I had to help him down the stairs and out onto the street. He'd dropped so much weight that it seemed like I could feel his ribcage when I sort of shuffle-lifted him down the staircase. He leaned against the old wooden pillars of the staircase while I went to get my car, the drizzle already dampening his thin hair.

But the damn car wouldn't start. I turned it over and over, over and over. Fuck! Cool outside as it was, I was sweating. What to do?

None of my friends lived very close by, and Roland was useless. I was three seconds from calling an ambulance, just what Drew would have abhorred, when the old Studey kicked over, and sat smoothly idling.

I pounded the steering wheel, and then ripped over to where Drew was standing, ghost-mask pale, against the stairs. We were at the hospice in a moment, and had a miracle: a parking spot. Drew had his paperwork with him; checking into the hospice was quick and easy. A very tall bearded man led Drew away after he'd signed some papers at the front desk, which was in a big foyer in the old Victorian. I couldn't see him after he went down the hallway, but I could hear his labored breathing. "Drew, I'll check on you later," I half-shouted, but he didn't reply.

And now I was an hour late for work. I was trying to do my best yogic breathing exercises, but because I wasn't a yogi, and in fact had never done any yoga, I was just kind of huffing a bit. Drew going in to hospice was a true downer, but I already knew it was only a matter of time. But I guess you could say that about any damn thing.

But I wasn't going to let the Studey choke again. I decided to drive it to work, and take a long lunch break down the Peninsula to see my best friends in the world, the fascist Studebaker mechanics, who had a monopoly on the Studebaker mechanic trade in these parts. It would almost be worth it to drive to Arizona to fix it rather than chum it up with those clowns. Funny, though—I was looking more forward to dealing with them than with Megan. I was really keeping strange company these days.

I parked in one of the crappy lots off of Mission and half-ran to work. I was whipping toward the door when I saw Jacob—Megan had taught me not to even think "Leg Man" anymore—leaning against the wall in his old spot. What the hell? I thought he'd left us behind for greener pastures. Crap, now I probably will have to talk with him about his daughter or some shit.

He actually nodded his head at me, but I pointed to the door and shouted, "Way late, catch you later!" and jumped in. I went right to my cube without looking up, but on my desk, along with a pile of fascinating leases to edit, was a Post-It from Megan: "Hayden, come see me right away."

Great.

I started to look over a lease, but couldn't even get the grasp of who wanted what, how many and why. It was in English, but I was thinking in Stress, a language all its own. Megan. Now.

I closed the door behind me in Megan's office without being asked. She looked up and smiled. "Hayden, did you miss your bus this morning? I know you don't often take the bus, but it is unusual for you to be so late."

"Yeah, had a little emergency this morning. OK now though."

"Oh, were you ill? You certainly don't need to come to work if you're ill."

"No, no, my housemate is pretty sick. But it's taken care of." I had been looking off at Megan's shelves behind her, but now I looked directly at her. She was hunched forward low on her desk, almost like a feeding animal. "Uh, so, what did you want to talk about?

"Precisely what we discussed on the phone yesterday. Jacob and his daughter." With her palms, she pushed herself up to a full sitting position, neck erect in her chair.

"Megan, really, I can't see how this can come to any good. I know Jacob's had some bad breaks, but we can't just interfere in his life. We barely know him. Sheesh, he's homeless; he begs outside our building."

Megan audibly exhaled through her nose. "Hayden, it's not as complicated as you perceive it to be. Yes, Jacob Reed is a homeless man, with some trouble. But he is a homeless man with estranged children. A homeless man, a father, that we actually know. This isn't like giving an anonymous donation. We could actually do some good here."

"But how? Look what happened last time! We can't—or at least I can't—be in the business of saving people from themselves. It's nuts!" I scratched the crown of my head vigorously and flopped back against my chair, which wasn't designed for flopping, and I almost fell over backward.

"Hayden, the problem last time is that I requested you to be the intermediary between myself and your former girlfriend, and there was too much emotional content between you two to have everything go smoothly. I am certain if you put me in contact with your friend—Sun is the name, I believe?—I'll be able to work something out between all the parties that will be mutually satisfactory."

"Mutually satisfactory?" I realized that I was almost shouting, so I held a breath for a moment. "Megan, this is not a leasing contract! These are *people*. Crazy people. Sun ... dammit, you have no clue. There's no way you can make this work."

Megan looked at me and said, very slowly, "Leave it in my hands."

I was about to protest, but then I thought about Drew, I thought about my lousy car, and I thought that I needed to slip away and get to my bullet-headed mechanics today. I gave up. I pulled a pad of paper that was on the edge of Megan's desk toward me and scribbled a number. I pushed the pad toward Megan. "Sun's number. Good luck. I have to get back to work."

I stood up and walked out, with Megan's measured "Thank you Hayden" hitting me in the back of the head as I exited.

On the way back to my office, I saw Diana walking out to the lobby, holding some folders. She was wearing a tight, pinkish knit sweater, and a longish skirt that was some neighbor to pink. She looked good. I veered over to her like I was magnetized.

"Diana, hey. Thanks again for coming to the party. How's everything with Mario?"

"Hi Hayden. I was just heading out to have an early lunch." She shifted the folders in front of her chest, which I hoped wasn't some kind of defensive ninja move. "Mario's OK. We had a weird little argument after your party. He was kinda, well, he was a little uncomfortable around some of your friends." She shifted the folders again, so they still covered her chest and a bit of her face too. "He liked you, for sure, and some of the other guys, but he thought some of you guys were pretty weird."

Involuntarily, I made a sound like I had passed a set of car keys. "Diana, no, nuh-uh, there's no 'you guys.' I'm not gay. That's just my roommate. And a lot of those other guys. And some of the girls too. But I'm not gay. I've never been gay." I could feel my face reddening, and I noticed that I was waving my hands a little.

She smiled without her teeth showing, and stepped back a step. "Oh. OK. So all those guys at the place, like the guy with the dog collar and those dudes dressed as guys, they aren't your friends? Your gay friends?"

"Well, yeah. I mean no. Yeah, I know some of them. They aren't exactly my friends; I've met them at other parties of my house-mate's, Drew. Drew is my friend. He's gay. They're all gay too. But I'm not. I just live there."

My last two sentences came out in a slightly high register. This was going well.

"OK, got it. It must be a little strange to live with all those gay guys. But that doesn't make you gay. I get it."

The thing about Diana was, besides the short skirts and all, she was smart, she was reasonable, she was a decent person. Clearly she didn't need to be tangled in my web, but spiders do as spiders do.

I sighed. "Diana, I don't live with all those guys. I just live with Drew. And Roland, the pervert with the movie camera, if you re-member. He's not gay. He's an alien. But I just live with Drew, and he's a great guy. He's pretty sick now though."

She nodded. "Right, OK. Hey Hayden, I did have fun at the party, but I really should get to lunch."

She turned and started to walk out, but since I don't have a big problem with bad timing, I said, "Diana, hey, why don't you and I go out? Like this Saturday? Maybe have a drink and a bite some-where?"

She laughed, a long loud laugh. But it felt like she wasn't exactly laughing at me. Or not completely. "Hayden, you don't have to try and prove you're not gay by asking me out. I mean, that's silly! I believe you."

"Diana, I've wanted to ask you out for months. This just seemed to be a chance, since we were already talking. And since I've proved I'm not gay."

She laughed again. "OK, sure Hayden. A drink and a bite. We can talk about the details later."

She turned and headed for the elevators. I watched the skirt move with her hips.

Maybe the day wasn't a total lost cause. But then I thought of my big victory in context with Drew going to hospice. Not exactly a balanced comparison; I've never been one for real balance. My monkey mind went back to the girl in pink, and my most pressing problem: A stalling Studebaker. I wasn't going to cozy up to a lease with any real passion today, so I decided to head down the Peninsula to my grease monkeys of little choice.

Out in front of the shop was a creamy canary-yellow (with white) two-tone Studey Golden Hawk, a bitchin' bit of automotive ice cream. Studebakers always went their own way in design—in fact, they were famous for a model that went both ways: the Champion, of which its peculiar bulbous front and rear ends caused critics to ask, "Which way is it going?" My Lark didn't have the exotic oddity of a Champion, nor the saucy speed of a Hawk, but it still had something going for it. Well, if you had a thing for Ramblers that had mated with an unostentatious but opinionated extraterrestrial.

Even if I couldn't afford the pricey Studey cheesecake, at least I was at the table. But now I was at the garage. One of the brothers came out of the shop holding some intestinal piece from an ailing engine, and nodded to me as I headed to the office. Inside, Bro #2 gave me a nod as well, looked out the window to see what challenge I delivered, and said, "Ahh, not just out for a Lark, are we? What's the trouble?" That was mechanic humor, if you don't recognize it.

I gave him a rundown on the stalling and sputtering and he took my keys and went out to the beast. Both brothers were immediately hood-deep; I could hear them laughing as they went after the rare bugs that only a Studebaker aficionado could squash, much less see. I relaxed in the office, which bore a big calendar with President Bush on it, a large American flag, a larger Confederate flag and an actual bust of Ronald Reagan. I was grateful that my incarceration lasted only 20 minutes, when Bro #1 came in; I could hear my car idling smoothly outside.

He held up a tiny darkened bit of metal, shaped a bit like a bullet. "This jet wouldn't fly. Lucky for you, we're the local source for defying gravity. Shouldn't stall now unless you drive it into the Bay."

"You're the man," I said. "In fact, you guys are the men. The men of Studebaker."

He crooked a glance at me while he rung me up, and then half-smiled. "Right," he said. The receipt, as usual, had a little NRA insignia on the top, with "Live Free or Die" quoted below. I figured if I ever wanted to outfit the Studey with a Gatling gun, I wouldn't have to search the phone book.

But even if those guys would have enjoyed having most of my friends from Santa Cruz put in cages, and maybe have Drew's friends roasted and served to the caged ones to eat, they knew their way around a carburetor. The Studey flew back up to the City. Diana, watch out.

Driving back, I thought of a great new angle on my *Karamazov* spinoff: my Alyosha character has some kind of horrible fever, after which he gets these prescient spells, where he murkily sees that the kidnappers are going to kill his father soon. But he can't focus in on where the kidnappers are keeping his dad, and the tension is escalating. I really want it to have a literary aspect too, so I need to have Dimitri writing a serious screenplay based on something like a lesser Eugene O'Neill work. Or maybe he turns a Beckett play into a kind of sex-romp comedy, but still literary. I'll have to work on that.

Thinking about what's next with the novel distracted me the whole way home, but once in the neighborhood, what was happening with Drew hit me again. Crap. And naturally I couldn't find a parking place to kill me. I drove around a full fifteen minutes, scanning even for totally illegal spots, but as with my neighborhood, the animals had already parked in front of the hydrants, and curling around the corners. Great.

I sat idling on Pierce, about six houses down from the corner crack house, just waiting to see if anyone would move. I was beat, so when this little guy opened the passenger door and got into and sat down, I didn't jump. He wasn't really a kid; but a pretty young guy, real short, with a big head. He held out an open palm to me, holding a little vial with a chunk of white in it. "Hey man, you wanna buy a rock?"

I couldn't help but laugh. I looked at his hand and at him and said, "No, not really. I'd love to buy a parking place though."

He looked up and down the street. "Yeah. This neighborhood's the shits for cars. Later." He popped out of the car and walked around the corner. It took me about five more minutes to find a spot two blocks away. I walked up the stairs into the house and was going to turn into my room when I saw Roland sitting on the couch, feet up on the gazing ball table. I did a double take. Those rare occasions when I'd catch Roland in the kitchen would have him scurrying like a mouse back to his room with his meager food. Roland, sitting in the living room?

"Roland, hey what's wrong? Is it Drew?"

He looked up at me out of a coat that was about three sizes too big for him, the collar tucked high on his neck. "No. Well, yeah. I mean, Drew's OK. Well, he's not OK. But I just saw him, and he's doing sort of OK."

I sat down in the big chair near the dead fireplace, opposite the couch. "You saw him? You mean he came back here?"

"No. I visited him at the hospice. He seemed surprised to see me. He said to tell you that everything's fine." Roland had a way of looking at your forehead when he was talking to you, but now he looked into my face, though he'd only hold my eye for a moment.

"You visited him? Wow! I mean, damn, it always seems like you're too busy with your stuff to be around us much. Huh. Well, that's good, I mean that's great you visited him. I didn't even know you knew he was sick, or that he'd made arrangements for the hospice."

Roland shifted on the couch, and seemed like he was starting to take off the huge jacket, but then he settled back down.

"Well, I've heard him coughing a lot lately. But we've talked a few times. You weren't here. He wanted to make sure I knew what was going on, and that we might need to find a new housemate and everything. He's very organized."

I leaned forward in the chair. My reflection in the gazing ball made me look like a wizened old man. "Yeah, shit, organized. For sure. Even now."

Roland got up. "OK. Talk to you later," he said, and then walked into his room and shut the door.

Talk to me later? That was the most he'd talked to me in six months. And Roland went to visit Drew before me? These were strange days. I'd just gotten one step into my room when the phone rang. It was Sun.

"Hey Hay-den. It's Sun. Are you busy?"

"Hi Sun. No, not exactly. Been a strange day though. What's going on?"

"Strange day here too. Karmic, maybe. These guys from the planning department came out today. They re-checked some structural stuff about the yoga studio, and it turns out the quake damage was more serious than they first thought. They red-tagged it. Looks like it might be months before it can be repaired."

"Oh, wow, that's crappy," I said.

"Yeah, so, Patricia, you know, the head of the studio said she might rent a place over on the Westside, a fancier place, until it's fixed. But I just had the feeling maybe it's time for me to stop teaching yoga, and to move on. Wait a sec."

I heard a sound like a chair scraping, and then she came back on. "Sorry, had to sit at the table. Trying this new soy/bulgar concoction. Supposed to boost energy. Anyway, remember a long time ago, when you said that you thought that I had a real knack for talking to and working with kids, after seeing me work in that day camp a few summers ago? Well, I was thinking about that, and thinking that I might want to go back to school, get some kind of children's counseling certification. What do you think?"

What did I think? I thought it was shocking that Sun was calling me for advice. That she remembered something I'd said casually to her years ago. "Well, yeah, I think that sounds great! I do remember how well things went in that camp, and how much fun you had. There are probably programs at the UC and at Cabrillo, if you haven't checked already."

"No, I haven't checked yet. I wanted to mention it to you first. I'll probably have to get some kind of part-time job, because the rent will be tight until I can find a housemate."

"Well, you never had a real problem finding work when you wanted it. But I think you should go for the counseling thing. It never seemed to me that yoga is your real calling."

"Right," she said. "And you know that I have to pursue a calling." She laughed, an easy melodious laugh that thrilled me more than I wanted it to. I took a deep breath.

"Um, Sun, I'm really glad you gave me a call, and I think you are absolutely right to move on from yoga. But there's something else: my boss, Megan, I've told you about her, she's the one who sent that message before about Tabitha's dad, right? Well, she's got herself all wrapped up in Jacob's, you know, Tabitha's dad's, welfare.

She might get in contact with you again on that subject. I'm not sure ..." I trailed off, expecting a bad reaction.

Sun didn't speak for a moment. "OK. That's OK. Tabby's been pretty down for a bit. I think it has something to do with her dad, or her family, but she won't talk about it. I'll wait to hear from Megan. Maybe I can help."

We talked for a couple more minutes and then hung up. It was almost too much to ask for: Sun actually asking me about her future, and then not blowing up about another episode around Jacob. This had been quite a day. And I didn't even need that crack that guy had tried to sell me.

TWENTY SEVEN

···

I t really is beautiful, Megan thought. I'd like to have it myself. He'll probably make some crack about it being American-made, but he'll know what a fine piece it is. She picked up the clock's brass key, but smiled and set it down again, because she'd wound it late the night before, and it wouldn't need winding again for hours. But she enjoyed the mechanical precision of the process. Indeed, the clock would have been right at home remaining at rest on Megan's marble mantle. It was a 1927 Seth Thomas, made the year that Megan's father was born. Its beautifully wrought walnut cabinetry was of a piece with the elegant numbers and dials on the clock's face.

Though the City had numerous high-end antique stores and specialty clock shops with quality goods, it had taken Megan two weeks to find the perfect item, and the one matching her father's birthdate. She listened to the clock's gentle ticking and smiled again. The jangling of the phone swept her reverie away.

She heard "Am I speaking to Megan Thornstock?" spoken in a deep, slow voice.

"This is she. How can I help you?"

"Miss Thornstock, I'm Sgt. Robert Billston of District D14 of the Boston Police Department. I'm sorry to call so early, but I have some bad news. Your parents were in a car accident last night."

The officer paused for a moment. "I regret to say that neither of them survived."

Megan reached out to the mantle to steady herself; the veins on the back of her hand stood up from the pressure she put on it. For a moment she thought she would faint; her hairline at the back of her neck became damp.

"Miss Thornstock, are you still there?"

"Yes."

"I know this must be very difficult news. We were able to contact you because your father had a business card of yours and an old letter of yours in his wallet. Do you have other relatives in the Boston area?"

"My father ... Relatives? No, no relatives."

"Well, unpleasant as this is, you'll need to call the hospital to release the bodies from the hospital morgue, and to make arrangements. Do you have a pen?"

Megan set the receiver on the mantle, and walked over to the secretary. She picked up a pen off the blotter and then sat down on the edge of the desk's chair. She shook herself a little, looked at the phone and got back up.

"Miss Thornstock, are you there?"

"Yes. I have a pen."

"OK. Again, I'm very sorry to have to give you this news."

Megan cleared her throat, but said nothing. The voice on the phone gave her a series of numbers, and then repeated them. She wrote them in scratchy block letters on the page.

"Please call as soon as you can. It was an apparently drunk driver that ran a red light; they didn't have a chance. From the flyer we found in the car, it looked like they may have been coming back from a play at the university."

"A play, yes," said Megan. "Thank you very much, officer." She hung up without waiting for a reply. She walked to the edge of her bed and sat down. She noticed it was cold in the room, but didn't get up to turn on the heat. The window looking out down Taylor was streaked with droplets from the morning fog, which had been whipped about by a brisk wind. Megan looked at her watch; it was time to get ready for work.

An hour later, she was still sitting on the edge of the bed. A memory had come back to her, but it wasn't completely clear. They were still in London, and she was only four or five. She had been riding a tricycle out in front of her parent's flat in Kensington and had fallen over. Her father had come and picked her up and had said something like, "Just a bit of a cock-up, my darling. No need to fret. All fine now."

Had he really said "my darling?" Did my father ever use that word? She couldn't remember him calling her mother "darling," though that didn't mean they weren't affectionate toward each other. They joked a lot together, in their own way. It was a blue tricycle. A little blue tricycle. Of course it would be little. He probably didn't say "darling," though that's how I remember it.

She hadn't cried at all, though when it began, it was as though her body was crying her. The pulsing, quivering sobs shook her shoulders violently, almost as though someone had her in a grip, and was vibrating her whole body. The white t-shirt she had worn to bed the night before was soon damp with tears, which had dripped down her neckline. Though her body was moving involuntarily, she kept her hands quietly clasped in her lap.

After a while, she got up and slowly walked into the kitchen. She pulled a tumbler off the glassware shelf, picked up a two-thirds full fifth of vodka from the counter, and poured several fingers of liquor into the glass. Because she was breathing heavily, almost panting, her first drink nearly came back up. She steadied herself on the counter and finished the glass, expelling a sharp breath after the swallow.

She poured herself the same amount, and quickly drank it. She poured herself another, drank half, and took it into the bedroom with her, sipping it while she got dressed. She finished getting dressed in concert with draining the last of the glass. Then she headed up to the roof.

It was blustery and damp on the roof, the heavy fog leaving puddles like those from a light rain. She walked up to the rose trellis, where the Father Christmas had flowered in a small flush mid-way up. She pulled hard at the main cane of the plant, but it only bent slightly. Then she moved to the side of the trellis and pulled sharply with both hands on two of the crosspieces, and the entire trellis came down, snapping the rose trunk. She stepped back and looked at it and then at her left thumb, which was bleeding from a small cut. She absently put the thumb in her mouth, and then started crying again.

Back in her apartment, she poured a splash more vodka in her glass and returned to her seat on the edge of the bed. After a few minutes, she went to the phone and dialed McManus at Consolidated.

"Mr. McManus? Megan here. I was a little bit unwell today, um, earlier today, this day. Late now. But I will most certainly come in, I'll come in now."

"Megan? You don't sound well. There's no need to come in to work when you are ill."

"No, is, it's fine, fine. I'll be at my desk quite promptly, soon."

"Well, good show, Megan. Cheerio and all," said McManus, who then hung up.

Megan got up, and picked up a piece of paper on the floor next to the secretary. It was the hospital phone number. She looked at it for a moment, and then set it back on the desk. She glanced up at her father's clock on the mantle and saw that it had stopped. She stared at the face of the clock for a long moment. My nose is running. I should bring a handkerchief. She wiped at her nose, walked into the kitchen and poured a short drink of vodka into the glass, downing it with one gulp. She left her apartment and headed down to the streetcar. I forgot my handkerchief, she thought while she waited.

When she arrived outside Consolidated, the heavy drizzle had stopped, but it was still overcast and cool. She slowly approached the double-doors at the building's entry, but when she was near enough to open one, she stopped. Jacob, she thought.

He wasn't panhandling outside the building, so she walked to the entrance of the alley. She saw him standing in the middle of the alley holding a piece of paper. When she'd walked a few steps in, he turned and looked up at her.

TWENTY EIGHT

....

*A*nd dad, I know you think that there's still a chance of working stuff out. But it's just been too long. Yes, we can talk now and then, and maybe even get together with Josh sometime, but not now, not anytime soon. Too much has happened. I am still your daughter, but too much has happened.

— Tabitha

Jacob had waited until he got back to the alley before opening the letter, given to him by Patricia at the bank. He'd held it in his hands during his walk back up Market, and waved it at Sully when he walked by, though he didn't stop to shoot the bull. No time for that.

Too much has happened, he thought. Shit, yeah. But we're still here. Five years without a drink. That happened too. That's something, isn't it? Tabby's mother's got her ear. What do I have? Shit.

He read the letter for the third time when he heard footsteps in the alley. He turned. Megan. Jacob had seen all the walks. Walking prim-drunk, like some proper drunks do, holding their chins upright and taking little chippy steps, one foot pushed forward and then the next, like a machine. She's blind underwater. Dead bombed.

Megan clicked forward, both of them staring at the other, no one speaking. When Megan came to within six feet of Jacob, he saw the flushed face and the swollen eyes. Nose running too. Messed-up.

"Megan, what in hell? You got to get back home, girl, and now! You shouldn't be out here like this. Are you coming from work?" Jacob stuffed the letter in his back pocket and moved a step toward Megan.

"My parents," Megan said. Her voice wasn't loud enough to be a wail, but it cracked in a high place, and the words were ejected from her mouth by a quivering breath. "They're all gone. Bad accident." She moved up to Jacob and came almost to his chest, looking up at him, eyes streaming.

"God, Megan! What? What was the accident? What happened?"

"A car accident. My father is dead. My mother dead. They're all gone." She pulled herself into Jacob's chest, wrapping her arms around his thick frame. She sobbed loudly, her shoulders heaving.

Jacob put one of his arms around her shoulders, and the other he wrapped softly across her head, with his hand in her hair. He looked up to see if anyone from the Market Street sidewalk was looking down into the alley. Good god almighty. Her parents dead? Maybe she's just so blotto she doesn't even know what's happened. Great. Some cop's gonna walk by and think I'm raping the white woman in the alley. He looked up the alley again, and then shifted on his feet and pushed Megan slightly away, putting his large hands softly on her shoulders.

"Megan, you have to get it together now. Let's take a breath here. Now tell me what happened."

Megan pushed her hand across her face, rubbing both under her left eye and her nose. She shook her head slightly and said, "OK. OK. I—"

Jacob's back was to the new alley occupants and Megan wasn't paying attention. It was only when the first man spoke that Jacob realized how close they were. The first man actually didn't speak first, but whistled loudly. If a whistle could sound derisive, his did.

"Check this, K. Old one leg has got himself the same sweet bitch that was here last time. This is like a family reunion."

It was the tall young black man that had robbed Jacob of his money and medals in the alley, what seemed like years ago. He was joined by the same short, ragged, very young Hispanic man, who this time held a long knife with a dingy black blade. The tall man waved the same small club, the short table leg that Jacob saw in their first encounter. But the thing that Jacob focused on was that the tall man wore his Bronze Star, and the short one the Purple Heart, pinned to their shabby coats.

"Shit yeah," said K. "But this time, we're going to have better family relations."

Megan had taken a step back from Jacob when she'd seen the assailants. The short man stepped forward toward her and put the knife-holding hand around her shoulders, pulled her toward him, and grabbed her breast with his other hand. She started to scream, but before she could finish, Jacob moved.

He lunged forward off his good leg and struck the short man a sharp, rapid blow with the heel of his palm into the man's Adam's apple. The man dropped to the ground like he'd been shot, making a loud, high-pitched rasping noise as he writhed on the alley floor. Jacob turned to the tall one.

The tall one waved the club above his head, but he stepped back a step, watching Jacob, wide-eyed. "Don't fucking think about it old man. I'll fuck you up! Back off!"

Jacob eyed him, and took a step toward him, moving his body sideways to his assailant's front. The man swung the club toward Jacob's head, but Jacob caught his arm and in a sharp motion, swung him around so that he had the man pinned from the back, one arm holding the club arm and the other arm around the man's neck. He choked him hard, the man's eyes bulging. In a moment, the man's eyes closed, and he slumped to the alley ground.

Jacob stepped over to the shorter man, who had continued to thrash around on the ground, his breath staccato and loud. Jacob bent down, looked at him, and tore the Purple Heart off his stained coat. He moved over to the tall, unconscious man, put two fingers on his neck for a moment, and then took the Bronze Star from his coat as well. He walked to his cabinet in the alley and came back with a rope, which he used to tie the unconscious man's arms and legs, making the knots in quick, easy motions. Then he turned to Megan.

"They'll both live. Though that one with the busted windpipe might not if he doesn't get a doc soon. Neither going to feel tip-top for a while."

He looked at Megan, who had stepped back to the alley wall when the fighting had begun, and was leaning against it, breathing hard. "Megan, I know this is a lot to ask right now, but you see that little crowd of folks that are at the head of the alley right now? Well, if I approached them, it might scare the shit out of them, from all this. I need you to go up to one of them and get them to call an ambulance and bring 'em down here. They'll probably want to call the cops too."

He looked up toward Market, where a group of five or six people, mostly men, some in suits, were staring down the alley at them. "Grab one of those boys in the suits; tell him you were attacked. He'll call."

He again looked down at the men on the ground. "I need to watch over our friends here to make sure they don't get into any more trouble."

Megan stared at Jacob. "Ohh," she said. "But ... are you okay?"

245

Jacob laughed. "Fine as I could be. A lot finer that these punks. Go get that guy in the grey suit; he's already wondering if I attacked you. Make him call. I don't want to see the cops down here, but the ambulance guys will call them anyway. Go!"

Megan stared at the men for a second, and then moved up the alley. She stumbled slightly when she first started to walk, but then righted herself. She was back in a moment.

"You were right. The man in the grey suit did think you were the attacker. His first words were questioning whether to call the police. I asked him to call an ambulance and he said he would."

"Good," Jacob said. "Now listen, the ambulance and probably the cops will be here in a few minutes. You can stay or go. I'll be fine. I think you should go, because they'll just ask a bunch of questions, and you're not ready for that, after the business with your parents, and this on top."

The short man had pushed himself up from the ground into a hunched-over sitting position. He was making a series of short, sharp coughs and a sound like he was crying. Jacob stepped over to him. "OK, you're going to be all right, but you have to try and breathe as softly and steadily as you can. Soft, shallow breaths. Just hold on; a doctor is coming," Jacob said. He glanced at the other man and saw that he was stirring a little, though his eyes were still closed. Jacob moved back near Megan.

"Megan, this is no time to be preaching, and I'm as far from a preacher as you got. But you got to look at the booze. Look at the booze here. It seems like it's a sweetheart, but it's just a chain. It will pull you down." Jacob took a deep breath. "I know," he said.

Megan looked up the alley toward Market Street. The regular street traffic had resumed, though the man in the grey suit was still at the head of the alley, looking at them and then looking up the street. "Yes," Megan said. "There has been some drinking. I thought it was fine. I'm not sure." She faced Jacob again. "But what about you and Tabitha? I had an idea that could be of help."

Jacob whipped his fingers through the thick gray-black mat of his hair. "Megan, please. No more. What will happen with Tabby and me is what will happen. No more. Get your own house in order." His face softened. "I'm very sorry about your parents. So sorry. You need to go home, and call a friend, and talk about it. Get off the streets. And do it before the cops come."

Megan's eyes reddened even more. "But that's why I came anyway. I wanted to talk about it with you. We are friends."

He put his hand on her shoulder and squeezed it slightly. "We are friends. We are. But we aren't that kind of friend, Megan. I'm just an old street bird, pecking here and there. That's not the friend for this. An old friend who knows you, that's the right friend. Make the call."

Megan nodded. She started to hug him, but he drew back slightly, and she stopped. He patted her on the shoulder again, and pushed her slightly in the direction of the street. She smiled at him and said, "Goodbye Jacob," and walked up the alley toward the street. He watched until she hit the sidewalk and turned up Market, away from Consolidated. Then he sat down on the ground, between the two fallen men.

TWENTY NINE

....

Megan rode the Muni home. The car was only half-full, though some of the aisle seats were taken up by packages. She'd forgotten it was Christmas Eve. She remembered how her parents would buy a huge number of gifts for her, and how she would madly rip them open under the tree. Toys and clothes and shiny things. But then her parents would leave her alone with the gifts.

One of the things that had later drawn her to the Bronte's writing was that they were sisters. Imagine—three talented writers in the family! But sisters. One of them a big sister. They could share secrets, be jealous of one another, laugh, compete, wake up in the morning to see one another all over again. And play with each other's gifts.

Call a friend. Jacob thought she should call a friend. But who? She'd been in sporadic contact with her closest college friend, Julie, but the last time they'd spoken they'd had a silly fight. She couldn't remember what it was even about. And Julie hadn't even known Megan's parents. There were some high school friends that did, but she hadn't spoken to any of them in many years. How could she even find them? What could she say?

The Muni car had stopped in an intersection because the overhead power-line cable had disconnected. The driver went out to reconnect it, but while he was doing so a street person began haranguing him, yelling something that Megan heard as "Phony, big phony." Or maybe it was "pony." The driver returned the car and muttered, "He don't know shit," and then resumed the car's movement. *I don't even have a friend here. Hayden. I could call Hayden, but what could he say? Would Hayden himself think we were friends? If you have to ask about something like that ...*

Megan sat up stiffly in the seat. *I need to make two calls,* she thought. *One to Consolidated and one to the hospital.*

THIRTY

....

Christmas Eve, yes! Work half a day, probably even get a little bonus in an envelope from one of the big boys—hey, maybe even some earthquake survival pay. And then Diana tonight. Maybe I'll get to unwrap my gift early. I'd always dug Christmas, even with all the crappy commercial stuff. My brother and I used to search the house for our presents—my parents' present-concealing security wasn't that great—and sometimes open them and rewrap them long before Christmas. But I'd told the folks I wasn't going to be down this year, and that was fine.

Last year I'd even gone out with Sylvie and Crenshaw to see the Macy's window in Union Square in all its glitzy glory. Of course, I'd had four shots of Jack Daniel's by that point, so I would have probably been amused by watching people walk up and down the stairs to the BART entrances.

But there was some weird pall happening in the office, particularly weird for Christmas Eve. I'd only gotten a few "yeahs" back from people I'd passed in the halls when I'd called out "Merry Christmas!" And I couldn't figure out what Megan was up to—I'd passed her office at least four times since I came in and there was no clue she'd even come in. She couldn't have an outside meeting on Christmas Eve, and she hadn't told me that she'd be out. Then again, I didn't know everything that was happening at Consolidated, and didn't care to.

But Megan's whereabouts weren't top of mind; Diana's were. I'd deliberately avoided going over to her cube. I know, really wussy stuff, but I had some unnamed fear that I might jinx our date or I'd say something stupid that would make her realize that she had to shop for pet food rather than go out with me tonight. Besides, I'd been busy with a fascinating lease for something like 1,000 folding tables and chairs for a convention of Methodists in Southern Cal. Real high-level stuff.

But it made no sense that Mr. Suave Guy Hayden wouldn't go flirt up his date at least a little before we went out, so I bucked up and went over to Diana's cube. Sylvie was kind of draped over one side of the cube, not really looking at or even talking to Diana, who was staring off above her computer.

"Hey kids, what's with the zombie action? Is this like the Christmas Eve work protest?"

Sylvie looked up at me and didn't say anything. Her eyes were red like she might have been crying.

"Hayden, didn't you hear?" Diana said, looking up from her chair.

"What? Hear about what?"

Diana looked back toward her computer again and then swiveled in her seat toward me. "About Megan's parents," she said.

"No, what's the big mystery? She said they might come out—is that why she's not here?"

"They were killed in a car crash last night, both of them. They're both dead," said Diana, and her lip trembled. Sylvie looked at me, shook her head, and went back to her cube.

"Shit, are you sure? Are you sure?"

"Yes, Mr. McManus came around to our cubes and announced it. You must have been in the bathroom or something. It's awful."

I stood there for a moment, started to go to McManus's office and then stepped back to Diana's cube. "Diana, that's about as bad of news as we could get. Damn, damn. I don't even know what to say." I started to get down on one knee in front of her to speak a bit more privately, but that felt strange, so I just kind of hunched over and said, "Look, do you think we should still go out tonight? I mean, are you OK with it, still up for it?"

She laughed a little bit and said, "Oh sure Hayden, I was looking forward to it. Yeah, this is terrible and everything, but we should still go out. Seven, right? You'll get me?"

I smiled and stood back up. "Seven it is. There's nothing quite like a Christmas Eve Studebaker for turning a girl's head." She smiled and nodded and I walked out.

Megan's parents. Shit. She'd talked about them some. I know she had a lot of respect for them both, particularly her father. And her mom annoyed her at times. Both of them dead, at once. It's unbelievable. I thought how I might feel if both my parents died like that, but I wasn't able to really create a picture for it.

I sat at my desk for a minute, took a deep breath and called her house. Just the answering machine. I called again about ten minutes later. Same. I picked up the Methodist lease and stared at it for a while, and then called Megan again. No answer. I got up to go over to talk to Sylvie and Crenshaw about it, but then I sat back down. Then I sat at my desk until about ten of noon, and walked out without saying goodbye to anyone.

My big plan for today, before the date, was to finish up—well, *start,* really—Christmas shopping for my folks, and maybe even pick up something for Sun. I never was much of a shopper, so my typical procrastination had caught up with me. I had sent a couple of cards out to some friends. I was also going to visit Drew. I'd seen him a couple of days ago, and he was pretty bad, but didn't seem that much worse than a few days before.

But Megan's parents, wow. I felt so tired.

So I came home and crashed, for hours, in my silent house. But before I did, I listened to the long string of "Drew, I heard the news ..." and "Drew, I know we haven't spoken in a long time ..." and even "Drew, what's up with your sweet ass?" on the message machine. Drew's close friends, and he had many, already knew he was in hospice, and where to reach him. But being the systematic guy that he was, when he'd become sick a while back, he'd started calling or writing old friends he hadn't been in touch with in a long time, to tell them what was coming. And he had a lot of casual friends, people from the bar, people he'd brought home from the bar. Some knew he was sick, some didn't know a damn thing.

So for the past week or so I'd been coming home to the message machine filled with sad voices or clueless voices, and I'd had to call them back and let them know what was what with Drew. Roland never even looked at the machine; he never got any calls. But I couldn't handle calling anybody back today to tell them there wasn't much of Drew left. Like I said, I was tired.

I woke up and it was almost five, which amazed me, because I usually can't sleep in the daytime. I felt better, and thinking about being with Diana tonight made me feel better yet. And then I thought about Megan, and that put some rain on my parade. I called her again—no answer. This time I left a message: "Megan, this is Hayden. I heard about the awful, awful thing with your parents. God, I'm so sorry. It's just terrible. Please give me a call when you can. I'll try you again tomorrow."

Tomorrow. Christmas. Not gonna be a pretty Christmas for Megan.

But I pushed that cheery thought out of my mind. My mind had to concentrate: At first, I was leaning to taking Diana to some fancy place like Masa's or Stars, but what did I know from fancy places? She'd had Mario plugged in for a while—she's probably done all the fancy places, and I'd probably mispronounce something on the wine list and give the whole restaurant something to smirk about. So I turned left on that idea: let's go funky instead of fancy.

She'd probably never been to Mission Rock, the bar and café out in Mission Bay near the old docks and industrial buildings. It was kind of a dive with spirit, in a part of town that wasn't yet getting a fresh paint job. But it did have views of the water, among the rotting docks. And though I'd only been a few times, they always poured their shots with a liberal hand. Food was edible too. Hey, this was inspiration: maybe Diana would glom onto the fact that I was one of the real people. And then she might glom on to me.

We arrived around 7:30 to a pretty sparse crowd. No big surprise though: it was cold and drizzly, and it was Christmas Eve. Most sensible folks were probably crowded around the fire at home with their wool socks on, looking at the bigger socks—stockings, that is—on the wall. Me, I'm here at Mission Rock with Diana, which is pretty off-the-wall.

The first thing I noticed was our waitress. Or more specifically, our waitress's breasts. They were substantial, and most of the substance was showing, because she was wearing a low-cut purple velvet dress, in the style of one of Santa's naughty elves. Big boots and big white belt and her bosom snugged up—and out—in this overlapping leather-thonged décolletage. Diana was wearing a pretty short, tight skirt herself (along with thick leg-warmers on this cold night), but it was a frock coat compared to this woman's getup. Dear me.

It wasn't like I was scamming on her—she'd come right to our table after we'd plopped down and put her hands on the table and leaned over to us and said, "Merry Christmas! How 'bout a few drinks? First one's free, courtesy of the owners, who are in Puerto Vallarta now. I'm Marla."

Without taking our order, before we could say a thing, she then walked back to the bar and started talking with the bartender, who on this cold night was wearing a Santa's hat and a black tank-top over his monster muscles. They appeared to be very good friends, because she then went behind the bar, where Santa Tank gave her a quick shoulder massage, which was easily done, because she was kind of leaning her butt back against him while he worked her shoulders at an angle.

Diana and I both stared. "Do you think the waitress is drunk?" she said.

"If she isn't, she's very happy," I said. "From the looks of things, everyone in here is very happy." The Mission had six or seven old, round wooden tables and wooden chairs. There were two other couples at tables, both younger than Diana and me. There were three people at the small bar, an older couple and a young guy with high, heavily pomaded hair. For having only a few people in the joint, it was very loud, with people throwing back their heads laughing, one guy even pounding on his table.

Marla swung over to our table and set a couple of shots of whiskey down, hard enough so they splashed a little. "Whoops! I could probably get Jake to come over and lick that up," she said, wagging a thumb at Pomade Man, "But you don't know him yet. Maybe later. Merry Christmas!"

Diana started to say something to Marla, but she was back behind the bar in a second, this time arm-wrestling with the bartender, who pretended to lose. Diana looked from them to me. "Wow, we didn't even order this! Should we drink it?"

I sniffed the shot and took a sip. Whiskey for sure. "Well, damn, why not? From the atmosphere in here, I think she's been giving whiskey away to everyone, including herself. And from the shine in his eyes, I think the big guy behind the bar has had a few too. Cheers!"

We clinked glasses and knocked them down. Diana made a circle with her lips and blew out a breath. "Hoo!" she said. I loved a woman who drank whiskey, and I loved them even more when they looked like Diana. When the waitress rolled by again, we ordered burgers and fries and a couple of pints, standard Mission Rock cuisine, but pretty good when I'd had them before. Marla returned first with the beers, plus two more shots. "Hey, we already opened the bottle of Jack. We don't want it to go stale, you know." She honked out a big laugh, set her serving tray on the table, and adjusted her breasts, which had been attempting to leave the last of their constraints.

We both watched her go back behind the bar. This time, she came behind the bartender and reached inside his tank top and rubbed his chest. He turned around and made like he was going to rub her chest, but he stopped mid-way and laughed, as did everyone at the bar.

"I get the feeling you like our waitress's outfit," Diana said, with one eyebrow raised.

I took a swallow of beer. I didn't know Diana all that well, and wasn't sure of my ground. But what the hell. "Well, she's very expressive. And generous. And yeah, her outfit: I guess she figured if she gave those things some air, they would stay fresh or something. It's a great outfit, for sure."

Diana smirked, and then she laughed. "You're right about one thing: she's as fresh as she can be."

We dug into our burgers. A bit later, someone kicked up the jukebox with "Wicked Game," a new song from local boy Chris Issak that was getting some airplay. It only took a second, and Santa Tank and Marla were out on the dance floor, which was this sort of open area in front of the bar. But they weren't exactly dancing. It was more like they were giving each other very friendly medical exams. She was running her fingers through his hair and then squeezing his ass and then back again, and he was returning in kind, and between stops adding a quick little roll of his hands over her generous chest. Then Pomade Man jumped out from the bar and sort of wrapped around her from behind in one big love sandwich. I looked at Diana; her face was flushed, cheeks in high red, and she was grinning a sloppy grin. She looked back at me and said, "Looks like fun, doesn't it?"

I hadn't realized that Diana was pretty stewed at this point. Multiple shots of whiskey will do that to you. I hadn't realized that, because *I* was pretty stewed at this point. So that when Diana grabbed my hand and pulled me from my seat, saying, "Let's dance!" I didn't really resist.

Both Santa Tank and Marla whooped when we came on to the floor, and so did someone from one of the tables. They whooped again when Diana raised one leg and halfway wrapped it around the back of my legs, while sort of hop-steppingly spinning me around a bit. I had to hang on to something, so I hung on to her hips, pulling her even tighter against me. And not being the most contained of men, I started to get hard.

The song ended to roars from all around. Tank, Marla and Pomade went back to the bar, and I did a bit of a crab walk back to our table, the "look the other way, I'm trying to walk like I don't have a hard-on" walk, with Diana hanging on to a belt loop on the back of my pants.

"That was fun!" she said. Her eyes glittered, and I paused for a second, looking at her red, full lips.

"Yeah, well, that was fun. I'm not a real dancer, but I guess that doesn't matter a lot here." I wiped my face, and looked back at Diana, who was staring at me with a loose grin. "Uh," I said, "Should we order some more drinks?"

"Nuh, I am w-a-s-t-e-d," she said, drawing out the word. "Maybe we should just head back."

Yes. Yes to anything. So I paid the check, which was about seventy-five percent cheaper than it should have been. I left Marla a big tip, but she hadn't even seen it when she came up to me and kissed me on the cheek at the door. She kissed Diana too, who just laughed. "You guys go unwrap your presents now. Merry Christmas!" she shouted, and most of the people in the bar joined in as a chorus.

When we got to the car, I was thinking about how I could go about unwrapping my present, but Diana wasn't working on theory: she was all over me. In a moment, we were tucked up against the passenger side door, and the windows were fogging. Even though the Studey is a pretty big box, it was fairly tight for two squirming adults. I hit the steering wheel with my legs a couple of times and suggested we get in the back seat. We clambered over and dug in.

There was a lot of sloppy kissing and squeezing; the car seemed to be 100 degrees. I worked my hand up between Diana's legs, and butted it up against her panties. I could feel her hot dampness, and moved my hand slowly over that sweet center, still outside her panties. She moaned, a long expressive moan, and since I was kissing her neck at the same time, the moan shot right into my ear.

And that's what did it.

Maybe it was watching Marla and her sandwich twins, maybe it was Diana's semi-dirty dance turning up my temperature, maybe it was because I'd been fantasizing about being in this very position with Diana for more than a year, maybe it was because I'd had four shots of whiskey and beer too, but I came in a shuddering thrust against her and let go an involuntary "Unnnhhhhh" against her neck, where my face was buried.

Came with my pants on, came before we could even make that delirious boy-girl gallop, came in the back of the old Studebaker on a wet Christmas Eve when lately, life seemed to be more puzzle than pleasure to me.

So. When a boy lets go, even when he's with his supreme love goddess, even when he knows it's time to continue to pay deep attention to her comforts and needs, it's hard—bad word—to maintain the full commitment, the ardor. I pulled back a little from Diana, and looked at her face, but not before I noticed that I'd left a small puddle of drool at the base of her neck. She had her eyes half-closed and her lips parted; in the dark confines of the car, with a bit of light from a streetlamp close by, her face had a pale glow. She was beautiful. And now puzzled.

"Hayden, what's with? Why are you stopping?" She lifted her head up and stared at me.

"Uhh, I don't know. This is great. I just, um, I think it was the burger. My stomach doesn't feel right. Maybe I should get some water or something. What if we just cruised back to your place and we could get comfortable over there?"

I even thought that sounded reasonable. I am a hopeful man, after all. But perhaps not that clever of one.

"Hayden, what the fuck? I mean, this was good. You were pretty damn into it. I thought we were going to rock and roll." She screwed her head to the side, a small sneer on her face.

Because I can always top off a stupid statement with a stupider one, and I didn't want to break my rhythm, I came up with, "Well, we rolled a little, but I guess we didn't rock." I pushed myself up from the seat bench and shifted to a sitting position, and laughed a little.

Diana pushed herself up and away from my leg, which had been resting on her. "So that's a pretty asshole thing to say, Hayden. I mean, you ask me out, we have some fun, we're getting together, and your little stomach starts to bug you? Just take me home, now. You can get water back at your house."

I made the usual noises of conciliation and apology on the long ride back to the Marina. It was foggy enough to essentially be raining, and in those spaces when I wasn't saying something lame to Diana, the droning wipe-wipe of the windshield wipers was the orchestration to my sad opera. I could feel the big damp place on my pants when I moved my foot from the brake to the gas pedal. She muttered a couple of "Yeah, whatever. It's OK, just take me home," to my blather, but finally I stopped talking, and we rode back in silence.

I stopped the car outside her house, and turned off the ignition. I started to apologize again, but Diana turned to me, hand on the door handle, and said, "Hayden, don't get into it; just leave it. I really don't understand guys sometimes. I'll see you back at work."

She got out of the car and headed up the sidewalk. I said "Merry Christmas" in a kind of a downbeat way, and she waved her arm back at me without slowing or looking back. She entered the darkened house, and I saw a dim light come on through dark curtains. Then I left.

Wow. So my ride to the top of the mountain was much faster on the way down. I drove back to the house, and shook my head a couple of times about what had happened with Diana. But weirdly enough, mostly my mind kept running back to Megan. She must have gone back East. Maybe she'll be gone for a couple of weeks, if she has to make arrangements for her parents' property and their belongings. But it was the holidays, so a lot of people would be gone from work anyway. I hoped she wasn't drinking heavily.

When I got home, coming up the stairs, I notice how cold the house was. It was *very* cold, like the windows had been left open. I checked the thermostat, but it seemed OK. I saw that the answering machine was blinking again, but I was too tired to deal with Drew's friends now. Maybe Megan had called as well, but that could wait too. I got into bed. So cold. It took me a long time to fall to sleep.

THIRTY ONE

....

I got up pretty early and put the coffee water on. Diana, man, could I turn a sweet situation sideways. I wondered if she'd ever go out with me again. Or what kind of looks I'll get in the office if she tells somebody else. The pot was coming to a boil when I saw the blinkety-blink of the answering machine on the little phone table we had in the kitchen.

It wasn't a bunch of Drew's friends checking for an update. Nor was it Megan returning my call. There was just a single message, and it was Rhonda, one of the Stardust Twins. Drew's friend. He said, "Hayden, it's Rhonda. I'm sorry, I called a few times. I wanted to talk to you directly, but this will have to work. Drew's gone. Drew's gone, man."

Here he choked up, and paused for a moment, and then came back, voice weak. "OK, so we knew it was going to happen soon. I organized a party a couple of weeks ago, I was stupid not to tell you, but we wanted to do it right after he went. Anyway, we're meeting at Ocean Beach around 48th tomorrow at ten in the morning. I hope you can come." He paused, and I could hear him breathing. "Drew loved Christmas, so it will be a party. I hope you can come." He hung up without saying goodbye.

Drew's gone.

I don't know why, but I went in his room and sat on the bed. I'd cleaned a lot of his mess up over the past couple of weeks, but there was still a big pile of clothes on the floor of his closet. I sat on the bed and looked at all his things, the stencil kit that he used to draw out his handmade fonts for his posters, his books, which had some literary classics mixed in with a lot of gay stuff, his wind-up toys, which were all over the mantle, the desk and on the shelf near his bed.

I wound up Minnie Mouse and set her on the shelf; Minnie moved forward in kind of a march, flinging her little round purse up in the air with each step. She jerked to a stop, and I picked the toy up and held it.

Drew did love Christmas. Last Christmas he'd decorated the entire house, with crazy streamers all over the living room and a dressmaker's doll that he made into a kind of unisex Santa. He bought a tree and did that old-fashioned thing where you string real popcorn, something I hadn't done since I was a kid, and he made handmade ornaments too, several of them obscene.

But this Christmas season, he was too sick to even begin. We didn't have anything: no tree, no silly Santa, just a lot of cards from his friends that filled the mantle over the fireplace. I'd been meaning to bring the cards to hospice to show him, but I hadn't gotten around to it. I hadn't gotten around to go visit him in the last few days either; too busy with work, too busy with my book, too busy with thinking about Megan and Diana and Sun.

The thing is, when I last saw him, I didn't exactly think it was the last time. I knew he was pretty close, but what did I really know; maybe he'd last for another month, maybe two. But he looked awful, and could barely talk, though he even told me a little joke about a stripper and he laughed. I held his hand for a minute, and told him that it was good to see him, and that I'd see him again soon.

But the real thing is, I wanted to tell him that I loved him. But instead, what came out was just "See ya."

Dead is a word that just falls to the floor and sticks. I sat on the bed for a while longer, and then got up, putting the Minnie Mouse in my pocket. I had to hustle to get to the beach on time. I got up and headed to my room to get dressed, but saw that Roland's door was wide open. Now that was truly strange. Everything was perfectly in its place, as usual, but it was like there had been an alien abduction: Roland never even left his door unlocked, much less open. But I had no time to ponder that.

At least it was vaguely sunny out for this sad Christmas. Cool, but with barely any fog at all. Though the Lower Haight can be a different weather world from the Sunset, out on the Avenues. But when I got there, it was still pretty nice. I almost wanted it to be a cold hell, but that's me.

I saw the group of people on the beach right off. Maybe forty people, men and women, a few older people in the mix. Nobody wearing anything outlandish except for a guy I didn't know with some incredibly tight canary-yellow stretch pants. A lot of people were standing around a fire of pretty big logs someone had started. I saw Meg, the manager of Drew's bar, a funny lesbian woman with a blonde crew cut, holding something above the fire. She was almost always laughing, but not today.

She was holding a stuffed toy, some kind of bird, above the fire. When I got closer, I could hear what she was saying.

"... and before I knew Drew at all, he'd brought this duck behind the bar and gave it a prominent spot among the bottles. I asked him what the hell that was, and he said it was his 'good luck duck.' I asked him what he needed a good luck duck for, and he said it might bring him a good luck fuck." The crowd laughed, but she kept a quiet face.

"I was going to tell him to get that crap out of the bar, but after that story, I couldn't. We all needed a good luck fuck. I always called Drew 'Ducky' after that."

And then she tossed the duck into the fire. People raised some plastic cups; I could smell some beer and other booze. I could see that there were some other things burning in the fire, some kind of doll, a little purple vest, a toy car, something that looked like women's underwear, but that was pretty far gone.

I looked around. I saw a lot of people I knew, mostly from the parties, a few from meeting other employees from Drew's bar the few times I went down there. I saw Donda and Rhonda, both dressed in black, standing together a little distance from the fire. They both nodded to me. Near me at the fire was a giant black guy, easily six-eight, who was holding a little framed sign that said "Even Queers Need Their Beers" out over the fire. I recognized from the lettering that Drew had made it.

The big guy was crying, and he spoke in a very deep but very soft voice. "First time I came in the bar, Drew was hanging this in the bathroom. I asked him, 'What is that shit?' and he told me this wasn't just a bar, it was an educational institution too. He looked at me like he was angry, then he laughed his head off. I was his friend from that moment on."

He threw the sign in the fire, and crossed his big arms, trying to staunch the shaking of his shoulders. Someone I didn't know patted him on the back. OK, now I get it—we were supposed to bring some artifact or something that connected us to Drew and throw it in the fire. Shit. I didn't have anything. But since I have that classic mind/body disconnect, I had to remind myself that I was holding, in my jacket pocket, the little windup Minnie Mouse I'd taken from Drew's room. That counted.

No one was saying anything, just staring into the fire—my moment. I cleared my throat and said, "Hi. I'm Hayden, Drew's housemate. I know some of you guys. I've known Drew for a couple of years ... I mean, I knew Drew, I got to know him pretty well. All of you know he could be a kind of a joker. He had a lot of toys that he sometimes played with like a kid. Here's his Minnie Mouse."

I brought Minnie out of my pocket and held her up by her little purse. "So, um, I wish Drew were here, because he loved a party." I looked around the fire and the faces and then down at my feet. "It's unbelievable that he's gone," I said, essentially muttering to my feet. Then I tossed Minnie into the flames.

The big guy clapped me softly on my back. I stepped away from the fire and looked around, and I saw Roland. He was twenty or thirty feet away, over by some big driftwood logs. He had his large movie camera out, with a tall tripod, and he was filming right in the face of Cory, Drew's bike messenger friend, who'd come by the house a couple of times. I hadn't noticed Roland at first because he had a weird get-up on, a long trench coat and an old-fashioned porkpie hat. What was he doing filming people here?

I walked over to him right when Cory was walking away. "Hey Roland, what's going on—what are you doing here?" I said.

He'd obviously been crying; he looked old, and even paler than normal. "Hayden," he said, and nodded. "I was making a small testimonial movie for Drew. Getting some statements from his friends. I wanted to do something for him."

"Well, wow, that's, that's nice. I didn't think you even talked to Drew too much."

He zipped the camera into a large leather bag and set it down against a big log. "Yes. Well, I did talk to Drew. He helped me. He helped me a lot. I'm gay, though I'm not, well, I'm not exactly active." He turned half away from me and looked out at the water, which was quieter than usual, just a soft shore break of small waves. "Drew and I talked a lot about that, about me feeling more comfortable about who I am. He helped. A lot."

I cleared my throat and looked out at the waves as well. Roland was gay? He talked to Drew? A lot? Man, I don't even know what happens in my own house. "Well shit, I didn't know you were gay. You know, we don't really know each other very well. But Drew was something though. A good guy."

Roland nodded, and turned to his equipment. He was crying again, but silently. He started to pick up his stuff and I said, "Well, I'd like to say something about Drew for the movie."

He smiled and took out the big camera, and quickly set up the tripod. I moved in front of it, and without giving me a chance to get settled, he said, "We're rolling."

I ran my fingers through my hair and looked at the lens. "Well, I didn't really know I'd be saying anything ... but Drew was my friend. He was the first gay guy I ever really knew. But that's not important. I mean, it was a big part of Drew's deal, but the important stuff was that he was a *real* guy, a giver. He helped a lot of people."

I yanked at my Adam's apple and cleared my throat. "This sounds stupid; I don't know what to say. What I mean is that he was my friend." I cleared my throat again. "I loved him."

I held up my hand to Roland, and he stopped filming. He wiped his face on the sleeve of that weird coat, and then packed up his stuff. "I'll see you back at the house, Hayden," he said.

Other people were starting to go. I stood there for a little while by myself, until Rhonda walked up with a tall vase of big flowers, gladiolas and birds of paradise and other flowers I recognized. They were the kinds of things Drew used to bring home from the Flower Mart, after they'd been in the bar for a while. "Hayden, hi. I'm happy you made it. Check these out, would you? Not quite as nice of an arrangement as Drew would have done, but it's darling, don't you think? I think it's fantastic you can get these flowers in the dead of winter!"

He looked up at me and patted me on the shoulder with his free hand. "We thought you might like to take these home, a little fanfare for Drew, my sweet baby." He turned his head a bit to the side and said, "Nothing of that funeral parlor taste in this vase, though. No dragons here, no coals, no coffins." He held the vase up to me and I took it.

My throat was closed, a tight ball. "OK," I said. He gave me a tiny smile and walked away. The waves were picking up a bit; there was even a surfer who was standing looking at the sets, probably wondering if he should just go for it since he was already here. I felt tired. Drew is dead. I clutched the big vase to my chest and walked back to the Studey.

I set the vase in the back, on the floor resting against the seat. I'd dumped most of the water. I headed back for home. Traffic was light; it was Christmas, after all. Not that it felt a damn thing like Christmas. I was on Lincoln, almost to the park when I thought where those flowers should actually go. Donda had said they didn't have any of that funeral-parlor taste, and maybe that made me think of Megan. Her parents.

Megan wasn't the type to like people dropping by her place, but what the hell. If she was still around, she was probably holed up, drinking, thinking of her parents and god knows what else. Me dropping by with some beautiful flowers couldn't make it any worse.

I was on the stairs below her apartment, lugging the vase, when this skinny guy wearing something like a Robin Hood hat, with a big white feather, came down.

"Well, here now, there's some Christmas cheer!" he said. He stopped one step above me, lifted his hat and dropped it back on his head. He winked and said, "That's a bouquet for a special friend if I've ever seen one."

I shifted the vase around to the other side of my head, so I could speak to him without flowers in my face. "Well, sure, not quite like that really. They're for a friend here. Do you live here?"

"Certainly do," he said. He thrust out a hand, which I took clumsily, having to shift one arm around the big vase. "Name's Turknot, Tuttle Turknot. Been here for a while, though I'm no native."

"Right," I said. "Well, these are for Megan, if you know her." I started heading up the stairs. "I should get going," I said.

"Megan," he said. He scratched his head. "Well, friend, Megan isn't here, I'm afraid. She's left."

"Oh, well, that's fine," I said. I'll just leave these outside her door."

He pulled his lips up in a weak smile. "Gosh, I'm sorry I wasn't clear. But I'm more sorry to say that Megan has left, for good. Or for bad, you might say. I'm sure you know about the terrible loss of her parents. She's gone back East. Gone home. Movers are coming to pack up the apartment tomorrow." He scratched his head. "Think it's available for rent now."

He backed up a little on the staircase railing and looked up the staircase toward Megan's apartment. "Had a beautiful garden up on the roof. We even talked about planting some corn up there. Not much left up there though. But Megan, she's gone."

I shifted the vase against the other shoulder, looked up toward Megan's apartment and blew out a long breath. "OK, well, that's good to know. I'll have to see if I can get in touch with her back there. I appreciate the information, Mr. Tuttle."

I started walking back down the stairs, and he shouted down at me, "It's Turknot, friend. Turknot's the last name. But you can call me Tuttle; all my friends do. Please tell Megan I said hello."

I sure would, Tuttle. I would if I was able to get in touch with Megan again, and if she wanted to speak with me, which wasn't all that clear now. But what did she owe me, really? I mean, we'd had some weird connection over the past couple of months that had been kind of intense, but that didn't mean that I should be at the top of her phone tree. Besides, her parents had just died. Drew too. Everything was dying.

On the way home, off of California, I saw a little girl wearing a Santa outfit, beard and all, that looked crazy with her long blond hair. She was walking down the street tugging a little cart with two littler boys in it, both of them wearing Santa outfits, and one of them was pulling what might have been a toy horse on wheels, maybe supposed to be a reindeer, behind the cart. I'd forgotten it was Christmas ten times today already. I slowed down to watch them and rolled down the window a little; she was loudly singing something I couldn't make out, and the boys were giggling. They weren't dying.

When I got home, I set the flowers on the living room table. They made a beautiful reflection in the biggest of the gazing balls. I sat on the couch and looked at them for a while. The sun had had been wrestling with the clouds, but it was in retreat. Early afternoon, and darkening.

Roland's door was closed, and I presumed he was in there, maybe even editing his film, but I didn't want to talk to him right then. But I thought about him making the film, wanting to do something for Drew. I sat there for a while, until it occurred to me that I could do something for Drew too.

I flipped on my little MacPlus, and punched up my novel. My plan took a lot of doing, because I had to introduce and integrate the Drew character in the early stage of the story, and also set up a little foreshadowing of his potential, without giving away anything critical.

My room was completely dark hours later, lit only from the glow of the small screen. But I was pretty happy with the setup. Drew was the answer to my story's dilemma: how to save the *Karamazov* father character from the kidnappers without it being his hapless family that saves him. Drew's going to be this guy that delivers flowers to the neighborhood where the kidnappers are holding daddy. The coke-abusing daughter is going to know him because she used to pick up her coke in the lower Haight where Drew lived, and they had casually spoken a few times before. So she'll have this crush on Drew, without knowing he's gay. I can work that one out deeper.

But the real deal is that Drew's going to catch the full implications of what's going on with the kidnapping, and instead of calling the police, he's going to burst in and free the dad, in a Bruce Willis-brand of macho glory. I will have to include some kind of back-story about him learning some martial art or something. But a significant part won't be any artificial focus that he's gay, but that he's a big, brave guy who isn't afraid of kicking some ass.

It sounds stupid and pandering, I know—push some kind of macho gay guy that's supposed to be the exception that proves the rule, whatever the freaking "rule" is, but I can write it so it doesn't come out like that. Write it so Drew's the regular guy, who happens to wear a rainbow wig now and then, and who sleeps with guys, and also makes dramatic heroic gestures. Hey, it's my novel.

But I hadn't quite written out all of the stupid in the version I had. But shit, that's what drafts are for. And Drew is in there, that's the important part. I shut down the Mac and sat for a moment. I was very hungry; I hadn't eaten for hours. I walked out to the kitchen. It was very, very quiet in the kitchen, and in our neighborhood. It was Christmas.

THIRTY TWO

....

Jacob took his time packing up the duffel bag. Sully had given him that big old fisherman's sweater, and now the bag wouldn't stuff down. First time he'd tried to put all his goods in the bag in a while. Backpack full too. He pulled the big sweater out and put it on, even though he was fairly warm already in his old coat. *Yes, better fit the bill. Old homeless dude in his layers, probably doesn't even know how many shirts he's got on. Keeps the tourists happy to see us wearing our houses.*

He pulled out the metal case that held the Bronze Star and started to put that into the backpack, but then he shoved it in the front pocket of his jeans, a tight fit. He opened the electrical cabinet door a last time, confirmed for the second time that it was empty, and softly closed it. He stacked the long cardboard boxes he'd been using for his between-the-dumpsters tent in a loose pile against the building wall, and tossed the two ratty blankets and sleeping bag, all of them torn and stained. Then he took a quick look around the alley and walked up to Market.

He turned the corner right when Hayden was opening the door to enter Consolidated. He hesitated for a second, and then he spoke, "Hayden, hold up there a second."

Hayden looked up, startled, and then let go of the door, looking at Jacob with an expressionless face. "Jacob, hey, how's it going?"

Jacob walked up to Hayden, and set the duffel on the sidewalk. "It goes, man, it goes. Hey, I want you to get a message to Megan; can you do that for me?"

"Uh, probably. I actually haven't spoken to Megan since the accident. She's not even here anymore, you know."

"Got that. I figured she wasn't going to stick around. And maybe that's for the best. But I wonder if you could tell her something for me. I want you to tell her that I'm moving into a little apartment in the Tenderloin. And that Tabby is going to visit me there." He smiled, a big smile, his eyes crinkling under the deep wrinkles. "Funny thing, didn't think we'd have any breakthrough, but she said if I got a place, she'd come and see me. So I did. Already met a couple of other folks who live in the apartment. They told me the neighborhood was kind of rough, and to be careful."

He laughed out loud. "That's a good one. They didn't know where I'd been sleeping for the past couple of years." His face turned serious. "Anyway, Hayden, you tell Megan that I'm here for her." He handed Hayden a slip of paper, on which was written a penciled telephone number. "Even got a phone! You give her that number, and tell her to give me a call if she wants to talk about anything."

Hayden looked at the paper and nodded. "That's good, Jacob. I'm glad for you. This is good."

Jacob touched Hayden lightly on the shoulder and started walking away. Just as Hayden was entering the building, Jacob said, "And tell her I'm checking *Wuthering Heights* out of the library. I know it isn't going to go all that well, but I have to know how it ends."

Leg feels good today. I could probably walk all the way to the park. Jacob walked up Market, moving easily through the hurrying businesspeople and the early tourists, his step light and true.

THIRTY THREE

···

What a trip. Now Jacob's going to give Megan advice. He really is a pretty good guy though. I'm glad he didn't know I called him Leg Man. I walked by Megan's office when I went in; it was antiseptically clean, a bright box of nothing. It was always tidy when Megan was in it, but this was different, the kind of empty that's cold.

The office was quiet. A lot of people took the day after Christmas off too, but I wasn't in the middle of any family travel, and I needed the dough anyway. I kind of liked a half-empty office anyway—fewer lawyers.

When I got to my office I saw the "From the Office of the Vice President" note, sitting neatly in the middle of my desk. McManus. I'd gotten a couple of these before, when I'd fucked up some leasing document by not putting a period after a lawyer's cough. But I'd never actually cost the company any money with my miscues. Only now maybe I had.

It was the usual semi-human note, written by his secretary: "Vice President McManus would like to discuss something with you in his office as soon as you get in." Well, at least I'd shaved. McManus's office was one of the bigger ones, looking out and down Market. It had enough height to look down into Justin Herman Plaza from an angle, and you could even catch a tiny wedge of the water too, though not on a foggy day like today.

McManus was standing and looking out that window when I walked in. "Excuse me, Mr. McManus, you wanted to see me?"

"Hayden, excellent! Good morning, good to see you!" He extended his ham-hock hand, which enveloped mine in its doughy mass. "Sit, sit, let's talk."

McManus had one of those giant desks that would provide ample cover for his big body should the National Guard come in and shoot up the place. He sat down in the high-backed dark leather chair behind the desk, while I took up a perch on one of the short swivel chairs positioned in front.

"So, Christmas OK? Anyone give you a sports car?" He guffawed, sending a little missile of spittle onto the aircraft-carrier plane of his desk.

"Not this time. But I'm open to it," I said.

He smiled, and then his round face went blank. "Hayden, the terrible circumstances of Megan's parents have put the company in a difficult position. She had taken a leave from the office—very understandable you know—but on Christmas Eve, she phoned and gave notice. She's not going to return to Consolidated."

He picked up a folder in front of him that had some paperwork in it that didn't need straightening and he straightened it, tapped the bottom edge of the folder on the desk, and then returned it to its original position.

"I spoke with Megan on the phone at length, and we both agreed that you are well-versed in the current state of the contracts she was managing. She praised the quality of your work, and your eye. Of course, you don't have the absolute background to step into her position, but we'd like to offer you a temporary stint behind Megan's desk, a probationary period of 60 days, during which we will find a suitable replacement."

He looked up and me and nodded in his best Colonel Mustard way. "After that, and if all goes well, we are prepared to boost your title and position here at Consolidated and give you more management responsibility over the other editors. Of course, during your temporary tenure in Megan's position, we will compensate you accordingly."

McManus smiled, picked up the folder again and set it down. "This is a fine opportunity Hayden. What do you think?"

I'd been focusing on the wainscoting for a segment of the time that McManus was talking. It was supposed to give the office some kind of dignified look, with its manly shade of dark cocoa and all, but I think this stuff wasn't oak or whatever hardwood gave wainscoting the gravitas, but some kind of balsa wood stained brown. There was a series of cracks and indentations at various heights on the walls—I think McManus had backed his chair against the wall more than once. Megan's office didn't have any wainscoting, for which I was grateful.

But he really had offered me Megan's job, hadn't he? I kind of came to attention, after having realized that McManus was staring at me, and I'd passed that tiny time limit of call and response that tells you that all the singers are in rhythm.

"Oh, sorry Mr. McManus. It's just that I was a bit startled at being offered Megan's job." I gripped the sides of the chair and straightened up. "What happened with Megan is just so sudden. And I was her friend too."

Weird move. I knew I shouldn't have brought anything personal into this, but McManus had opened a trapdoor under me by offering me the job. What? Me be Megan? I had a quick vision of a weighty day planner and some sensible suits. But the cash. The cash did call to me on a hotline.

McManus cleared his throat. "Yes. It is a tragedy. And we will sharply miss Megan. But we have to gird our loins and move forward, because Consolidated, even though it's a family, it's a business too."

Amazing—McManus was able to put girded loins and the family matters of Consolidated into a few sentences. I sidestepped—or swerved with a vengeance—from thinking of McManus's loins, and leaned forward. "Well, Mr. McManus, it's flattering to even be considered for the position. I wonder if I could think about it overnight, and come back to you with an answer in the morning?"

McManus gave me a few "Jolly Goods" and "By all means" and several other flavors of "OK, fine, out of my office" and shooed me out. I think he missed Megan—he was trying his lame Englishisms on me, but I couldn't muster up the subtle derision that Megan seemed to be able to summon at will.

But me, taking over her job? Groomed for management at Consolidated? Things were getting curiouser and curiouser.

I left early, but I didn't want to go back to the house. I actually found a parking place right up the street and then walked over to Toronado for a beer. That beer turned into many beers, over a long stretch of hours. I woke up out of a haze, staring at one of their black and white TVs that were always turned to static. Probably time to wobble home, so I did.

THIRTY FOUR

....

The next morning was cool and grey, but at least there wasn't any sharp wind. I walked up Market, which seemed quiet for a business morning, thinking of Jacob. My usual walk skirted the Tenderloin; there was a skinny black woman with a small Afro, a prostitute, whom I saw regularly out by the freeway overpass. We sometimes nodded to each other. She always wore shimmery miniskirts of some metallic-looking fabric, even in the cold, and she seemed too old to be doing what she was doing. I wondered where in the Tenderloin that Jacob might have moved; he'd probably start nodding to that woman too, and maybe even give her some advice.

Megan had made her move as well. Both of them had made moves, part of which were related to me in some weird way. Jacob's sounded pretty positive, but I wondered about Megan. I passed by the old Woolworth's building, and I looked around for the Prophet, but he wasn't out. I wondered if he had moved on too.

That's when I decided about the job. Nope. Wasn't going to do it. In fact, I wasn't going to do Consolidated any more, no Megan's job and no king bee of the proofreaders either. I didn't have anything to move toward, but I did have something to move away from, and I was going to make that move. The decision came to me like turning a key.

I went to my office, and looked over the stack of leasing documents. The client companies had names like "Associated Entities" and "Amalgamated Interests" and "Eastern Investments." The companies all needed objects to lease, engines of commerce, things to fill spaces. It was, and always had been, gibberish to me. I set the papers down and went to McManus's office.

He was resistant at first, sprinkling in some additional sugar on the cake, suggesting bonuses and hints of some kind of sharing in a larger pie, added prestige—there might even have been an intimation of wainscoting. But when I said I wanted to leave my old job too—today—he tried to lay the hammer down. He ranted a bit about company loyalty, blots on resumes, poor recommendations, and then he gave up.

He actually looked relieved. I think all along he suspected that I wasn't Consolidated material, and he was right. I told him that Sylvie could easily slip into my job, that she had all the smarts, and that Crenshaw would back her up. Hell, Crenshaw might not even leave her cube. We shook hands, and he wished me good luck, and I think he meant it too. I meant it right back at him—why not?

I shocked Sylvie when I told her, but she gave me a warm hug. Crenshaw gave me a little man hug; he actually looked like he might cry. Diana—Diana she was funny. She laughed, saying I was joking, then shook her head and asked if it had anything to do with the other night, and laughed again. Then she said I was joking again, and when I said I wasn't, she looked hurt. But she stood up and gave me a long hug, and even a kiss on the lips. "You can still call me, you know," she said when I started to walk away. I *didn't* know, but I was glad she said it.

I even said goodbye to one of the lawyers. And then I was out the door.

Somewhere near 4th, I heard some long sweet tones of a saxophone from some hidden building alcove. Probably some bum, cadging for a quarter, but definitely a talented bum. Kind of like me. Maybe I could take Jacob's spot at Consolidated. Probably better than proofreading leasing documents. But it felt pretty even keel to leave my job, without another one in the back pocket. Maybe I'd feel different tomorrow, but right now, it's cool.

When I got home, Roland's room was cleaned out. I mean *clean*: he'd mopped the floors for sure, and it looked like he'd even scrubbed the walls. Nothing left. Except for a note in the kitchen, which read:

Hayden, I know this is sudden, but Drew's death has really pushed me. I have an opportunity to go to a small film school outside of Los Angeles, and I've decided to go there a few months early. I'm sorry I didn't tell you this in person, and that you are going to have to be the guy to deal with the landlord and new renters, but I'm not all that good with goodbyes and personal details.

I wish you the best, Roland.

Whew. So the house is really filled with spirits now. Or just dead, flat air. I sat with Roland's note on the couch and read it a couple of times. I guess we all aren't that good with goodbyes. So it was helpful that Megan called right then.

"Hayden, good afternoon. I'm a little surprised to reach you; I thought I'd get the answering machine."

I was surprised by the strength of my reaction to Megan's call. One of those emotional stews, happy, sad, thick, thin, senses tingling. "Megan! Gosh, I'm glad you called. No, I left work early today. In fact, I left work." My voice trembled a bit while I was talking, but Megan's was trembling even more.

"Well, Hayden, I was able to retrieve the messages you'd left for me on my machine. I'm sorry I didn't answer you right away." She paused for a moment. "After my parents' crash, I had a few difficult days. I made some quick decisions, and I regret not informing you of them. I'm sure you know now that I've moved back here for good."

"I do, yes. I wish we had talked, but listen Megan, I really want to say how sorry I am for your parents and everything."

She didn't say anything. After a moment, I continued. "That is a truly awful thing. I hope everything's better—I mean, I hope you're able to get kind of settled, through all of this."

"Things are more clear. I am staying in my parents' place, but not for long. I've actually started a new job at my former company, which may seem stupid, but really, it's better than not."

"Yeah, well, I stopped working, as of today. I decided to quit. It's pretty crazy: McManus offered me your job for a couple of months, while they looked for a replacement. He was all, 'the company can guide you through this transition, Hayden,' but all of it seemed bogus to me."

I'd tried to imitate McManus's bass drum of a voice, and I must have done it well, because Megan laughed a real laugh, which took a melodic little climb in tone.

"McManus! That dreadful man. But Hayden, I'm alarmed that you quit. I hope you have another job in mind."

"Not exactly. But it's fine, really. But I have some good news: Jacob has moved into an apartment, in the Tenderloin. His daughter has said she's going to visit."

"Hayden, that's excellent news! Very good. So, you spoke to Jacob?"

"Yeah, and he wanted to make sure that you got his number. He said he'd be happy to hear from you anytime. He wanted to make sure you understood that."

I think Megan drew the phone away for a second and covered the receiver; I heard what might have been a stifled sob. But she quickly came back on. "Well, that's fine. Give me a moment to get a pen and paper."

I gave her Jacob's number, and she gave me hers. We chatted a little while, and then it seemed time to close it out. I started to say goodbye, when Megan chimed in: "Hayden, the company is much more open to commercial fiction now. We have expanded our list considerably since I last worked here. If you get your novel in shape, I can certainly put it in front of the proper editor."

"Wow, that's the best news I've heard in a while! Absolutely! I'm probably four chapters from finishing, and it's changed a fair amount from how I last described it. I think it has more emotional texture. Still wouldn't be what you—well, *you* in particular—would call a classic, though."

She laughed. But then I remembered what Jacob said. "Hey, before I go, let me tell you that Jacob said he was going to check out *Wuthering Heights* from the library. He had to finish it—for you, I think. Hell, maybe I'll even read it sometime."

I think she might have been crying; I'm not sure. But she said, softly, "That's good to know, Hayden. You take care," and hung up.

I thought maybe I'd heard the telltale clink of ice in a glass, but I wasn't sure. I'd been listening to the rise and fall of her voice, almost straining to hear the splash of liquor in her tones, but I just couldn't tell. I hoped she'd had a truce with the bottle.

It was getting dark very early now, and even though it was just late afternoon, the house was shadowy and grey. I went through the entire house, turning on lights, even in Drew's room. Even in Roland's room. Then I flipped on the Mac, went to the kitchen and poured a shot of Jack Daniel's, neat. I had another idea for the novel, and I had the time to work on it.

THIRTY FIVE

....

I t was weird to be in the house, Drew's house, with its outlandish colors, a lot of his furniture, and quirky things that
were pure Drew, without Drew there. And he wasn't coming
back. That's the really weird part. But his stuff also gave me a focus
for the next few days. I had Rhonda send the word out about Drew's
things being up for grabs, so for the next couple of days, there was
a parade of characters, most of whom I knew, coming by for books,
the desk, the toys, the bed and a couple of the smaller tables, one
from the kitchen, one from the living room. The big couch and
chair weren't Drew's, but I left his gazing balls on the living room
table—he was always fussing over them, and I thought they should
stay, reflecting the crazy colors of the room.

I only kept one thing: a wax stamp of his, that he used on his
hand-lettered correspondence, where he'd break out his self-de-
signed fonts, nice paper, and seal the envelope with the stamp. The
stamp was pewter, or some heavy silverish metal, and it had some
kind of old-timey soldier on it, from wars of another day. The
solider carried a rifle over his shoulder, and was wearing something
that looked like a kilt. Drew loved it: "My kind of soldier! One who
wears a dress," he'd said.

The imprint the stamp left was some kind of stylized "D," which of course Drew said was designed for him. And so it was. The soldier was sort of a good-luck charm for him, though I can't really judge how good Drew's luck was. But the stamp had something of Drew in it or on it, so I took it.

I called the landlord, told him about Drew and about Roland, and he said he'd pay for an ad in the paper advertising the rooms, and that I could choose the housemates. Didn't sound like much fun, but what could I do? So, the rooms were clean, the house was clean. I did look at the job classifieds a couple of times, but didn't see anything that I was qualified for. And gazing stone-eyed at legal documents again wasn't an option.

****

New Year's Eve morning. I got to do something that I hadn't done for a while: I biked through the park to Ocean Beach, and up over Lincoln, with its big-blue views, past Baker Beach and onto the bridge all the way over to the Marin side. I lucked out: the bridge was only slightly foggy and not very windy. I got to look back over the Marina and to downtown, and see soft light falling on the big buildings. The City had its velvet skirt on.

I thought about rolling into Sausalito, but I hadn't made the ride in a while, and I knew I'd be dragging on the way back. Back at home, there was the question of New Year's Eve night. I vaguely thought about calling Diana, but it was too soon. I probably could have even got a small Consolidated office crowd to hit some bars, but that also felt like bad timing, like I couldn't let go or something. The office was no longer mine.

I ended up shooting the Studey over to Edinburgh Castle, the old Scottish pub off of Geary. I even found a parking place without sweating. The place was packed, so I had to stand as I went through the greasily good fish and chips, a couple of beers and some single-malt I'd never heard of. I did raise a few toasts with some boozy new comrades, but I just didn't feel like hanging out until midnight, so I was back home by ten-thirty.

At ten-forty, Sun called.

"Hay-den, Sun. Happy New Year's! Can you talk?"

She sounded eager, excited even. Sun could always infect me with her mood, instantly. I took her up on it: "Happy New Year to you, girl! How come you're not out partying?"

"Stuff to do. Getting the house together. In fact, that's why I called. You know, I needed to find a housemate after Steve moved out, remember?"

Oh yeah. I remembered Steve and his backyard mirror-trick very well. "Yeah, right. What happened?"

"Well, nothing. I mean, I interviewed like ten people, and they were all losers. It's a real drag to try and figure out who will work out, and they're basically faking who they are when they interview you, and you're kind of faking your best self. It sucks."

"No doubt. So, what are you going to do?"

"Well, it's kind of like what *you're* going to do. Here it is: I'd like you to move back in. I mean, will you? Not as my instant boyfriend or anything, but because we know each other, we know about living with each other." She hesitated, and then said, "I dunno. I've always sort of thought I didn't actually need other people. But I do. We could possibly even make the house thing work, if you avoid being an asshole now and then."

I laughed loudly, and it felt good. "No promises," I said.

She laughed too. "I know you've got your job and everything, but I could probably hold out for a couple of months here on rent, and you could check out the Cruz for work over the next while, and make it down when you're ready."

I paused for a beat. "Weirdly enough, I don't have a job anymore. I don't have housemates anymore. And though I love the City, I don't have a real reason to be here anymore." I thought about it for a second, and that's all it took. "I'm ready now."

That's how it came to be that on New Year's Day, I drove down to Santa Cruz to talk about the details. The first detail of note is that when Sun answered the door, she gave me a real kiss, even with a little tongue. Then she cautioned me not to get any ideas. Me?

Yeah, I had to call the landlord all over again, and it's going to be a huff to get my stuff down in the Studey, but I can manage that with a couple of trips. I'll just give away any of the big stuff I won't need. It's a new year. I've got the novel, and Drew's soldier with a dress and maybe even Sun too. I'm set.

THIRTY SIX

....

Downtown San Francisco, Market Street, the first week of a new year. If you walked past the beautiful old Flood building, you'd probably notice the very tall, white, bearded man with the impassive face, leaning against the wall. He was obviously a street person, but self-contained, a planet with his own gravity. It was easy to believe that some locals might call him the Prophet, for his see-through-the-earth look, and the way he stretched out his huge hand for whatever a passerby might drop in, not seeming to care if anyone bothered. He wouldn't look your way when you passed, but he would have seen you.

Down just a couple of blocks, in a deep alcove made by the inset entryway of a bank building, a skinny, older black man lifted some blended notes from a dirty saxophone. He was playing a Coltrane blues, a ballad that pushed and pulled notes from a deep place. The man, Dexter, had his eyes closed and his head lifted up, and you could be forgiven if you thought the man and the music had melded into a kind of prayer.

Up high on upper Market, but not quite as high up as Consolidated Leasing, a tourist couple was consulting a map, looking around with confused expressions on their faces. A Muni train came rumbling past, deep and loud, and the tourist man made a quick, involuntary crouch. He knew there had been a big earth-quake a couple of months back, and he thought he'd had the bad luck to be in beautiful San Francisco with his wife when another big one struck.

He pointed to the Muni and laughed, and his wife laughed with him. This day, there would be a fine lunch, a nice stroll down the Embarcadero to Fisherman's Wharf, and a good dinner back in their hotel. This day, they would rely on themselves, and, without really knowing it, the kindness of strangers, and they would be re-warded.

This day, there would be no earthquake.

Can You Take a Moment for a Review?

If you enjoyed the book, I'd be grateful if you'd review it on Amazon or Goodreads. Respectively, go to www.amazon.com and/or www.goodreads.com and search for *Aftershock* after you arrive.

(Of course, reviews only need to be a few sentences or so, but do elaborate if you're of a mind to. Even if you thought the work was birdcage lining; I'm tough, I can take it.)

Thanks, and happy reading and writing to come!

Acknowledgements

To the city of San Francisco, which had the good sense not to completely fall down when that damn quake hit. To all my writing teachers, mentors and peers, who never assailed me with cruel remarks (though I glimpsed them looking askance when they thought I wasn't looking).

To the great writers of the world, who have shown me what to aspire to, damn them. And to my mother, who through the example of reading for pleasure, let me see that reading is traveling to other worlds.

ABOUT THE AUTHOR

Tom Bentley lives in the hinterlands of Watsonville, California, surrounded by strawberry fields and the occasional Airstream. He has run The Write Word, a writing and editing business, out of his home for many years, giving him ample time to vacuum.

His business projects have varied from writing website content, the full spectrum of marketing material, user documentation for software manuals, radio ads, character dialog in video games to editing coffee-table photography books.

He's published hundreds of freelance pieces—ranging from first-person essays to travel pieces to more journalistic subjects—in newspapers, magazines, and online. (Venues include *Writer's Digest,* the *Los Angeles Times, Writer's Market, Wired,* the *San Francisco Chronicle, The American Scholar,* and many others; he's also won a number of nonfiction writing awards.)

He's published short fiction in a number of small journals, and was the 1999 winner of the National Steinbeck Center's short story contest. His coming of age novel, *All Roads Are Circles,* was published in 2011. His short-story collection, *Flowering and Other Stories,* was published by AuthorMike Ink in early 2012. His corral-your-writing-ideas-and-get-them-to-the-page book, *Think Like a Writer: How to Write the Stories You See* was published in 2015.

His newest novel, *Swirled All the Way to the Shrub,* set in Prohibition-era Boston, was published in late 2018. *Shrub* is a collaborative novel written with Rick Wilson. Check out www.swirledshrub.com for details on the book's historical references, info on the collaborative process, and free resources related to the book.

Sign up for his writing-related newsletter and see his lurid website confessions at www.tombentley.com.